Caro was an infuriating woman

"I am not going in there, and you can't make me," Caro shouted at Gil, glaring into his face.

"Oh, yes, I can," said Gil with a mocking smile. Caro mutinously set her mouth and began backing toward the car. He still held on to her waist. She felt a strange flutter of pleasure, conscious of the warmth of his hands pressing upon her body. It was a possessive hold and she wanted to yield to it.

"You are a stubborn woman."

"You are a stubborn man," she retorted, and Gil laughed shortly.

"And you've always got an answer, haven't you?"

"If you mean I won't let you bully me and get away with it, then yes."

Then before she had time to turn her head, Gil bent and took her mouth in a hot urgent kiss.

CHARLOTTE LAMB began to write "because it was one job I could do without having to leave the children." Now writing is her profession. She has had more than forty Harlequin novels published since 1978. "I love to write," she explains, "and it comes very easily to me." She and her family live in a beautiful old home on the Isle of Man, between England and Ireland. Charlotte spends eight hours a day writing—and enjoys every minute of it.

Books by Charlotte Lamb

CHARLOTTE LAMB

the threat of love

Harlequin Books

TORONTO • NEW YORK • LONDON
AMSTERDAM • PARIS • SYDNEY • HAMBURG
STOCKHOLM • ATHENS • TOKYO • MILAN

Harlequin Presents first edition February 1992
ISBN 0-373-11435-4

Original hardcover edition published in 1990
by Mills & Boon Limited

THE THREAT OF LOVE

CHAPTER ONE

SEVERAL daily newspapers carried it on their front pages. It was hardly world news, but when two famous men had a fight in a nightclub Fleet Street was fascinated, especially if one of them was an earl.

Gil scowled down at the photograph while he ate his breakfast. Unfortunately, dim though the light had been in the nightclub, you could still recognise the faces, all of them well-known. Some of his friends had been laughing, but he hadn't. Black hair, black eyes, angular features taut with rage stared back at him. He was wearing evening dress, but under the smooth jacket his muscles showed. I look like a thug! he thought, throwing the paper across the table. Why, oh, why did a photographer have to be there?

He heard the telephone begin to ring—the Press again, no doubt. They had been trying to talk to him since early this morning. His staff knew how to respond to such calls: 'No comment,' was always the answer when the Press tried to speak to him. He had a public relations department who talked to the Press. Gil never did.

There was a tap on the door, and he glanced up, frowning. 'Yes?'

'Lady Westbrook on the telephone for you, sir.'

Gil had been expecting this call some time during the day, but not yet, because his grandmother usually got up quite late, and he was startled into betraying his surprise, his voice sharp. 'Already?'

Mrs Greybury was too discreet to let a flicker of expression cross her bland face. A woman of nearly fifty, with neat, greying fair hair and pale blue eyes, she and her husband had worked in foreign embassies for years before coming to work for Gilham Martell, and ever since their arrival his home had been run like clockwork. He had learnt to trust them both implicitly, and to rely on their discretion.

'I just left for the office, Mrs Greybury,' he decided, avoiding her eyes because he didn't like anyone knowing how much his grandmother overawed him. Most people who knew him would have insisted that Gilham Martell was nervous of nothing and nobody. They didn't know his grandmother.

'Should Lady Westbrook transfer the call to the car phone, sir?'

Gil got to his feet with an impatient lunge. 'No, tell her to ring the office.' He couldn't face one of her lectures—it was too early in the day, and especially after last night. He had a dull headache behind his temples; he hadn't had enough sleep. If he told his grandmother so, she would merely say it served him right, and perhaps it did, but he was in no mood to be told so.

It had hardly been his fault Colin had got drunk. It had been Miranda's birthday; she had given a dinner party at one of London's top restaurants, and then they had all gone on to a nightclub, around a dozen of them, all old friends. She had drunk too much, everyone had; they had all been in a reckless, excitable mood. That wouldn't have mattered if Miranda's husband hadn't decided to take offence at the way they had been dancing, cheek to cheek, body to warm, languid body, Miranda's arms tight around Gil's neck.

Typical of Colin! He was normally a mild, easy-going man, but when he drank he got macho and aggressive, chucking his weight around and remembering that his ancestors had been earls for three hundred years. It was always happening at parties; Colin was famous for it, and always deeply apologetic next morning, as, no doubt, he would be today.

If only that photographer hadn't been there, snapped them, and sold the picture to the gutter Press!

'Has John brought the car round?' he asked curtly.

'It's outside now, sir.' Mrs Greybury waited until she had heard the front door slam before she returned to the telephone. 'I'm sorry, my lady,' she said, glancing through the hall window to watch the black Rolls-Royce glide past. 'I'm afraid Mr Martell has already left for the office, if you would like to try there.' It was the truth now, after all!

Lady Westbrook made a seething noise. 'I suppose he just bolted out of the front door? I'll talk to him if I have to go down to the office to do it!' She hung up and Mrs Greybury slowly replaced her receiver, amusement in her eyes. She would love to be a fly on the wall at that confrontation! Gilham Martell and his grandmother were so alike, in looks and character; each knew precisely how to infuriate the other.

Tall, sparely built, they had the same bone-structure, the same eyes. Time had turned the old woman's hair white and withered her skin, but she still had an impact on those she met; always totally assured, her mouth could curve into a smile of charm and enchantment, and although she was in her eighties she still moved with grace. Plenty of people found Gilham Martell a tough man to deal with, but his grandmother ordered him about as if he were still a boy. If she had been asked to bet on the outcome of a clash between them, Freda Greybury's money would be on the old woman. For one thing, she had been alive for a long, long time, and because of that was tougher and even more used to getting her own way; and for another she had less time ahead of her than her grandson did. She was in a hurry to get what she wanted, and couldn't bear to be crossed. There was another reason—Gil Martell loved his grandmother dearly, and was in awe of her, which meant that she had him at a disadvantage whenever they quarrelled. He could never bear to upset her.

Irena, Lady Westbrook, sat upright in her stiff Victorian armchair, staring straight ahead, her mouth set. 'This time I am not going to let him talk his way out of it! Disgraceful behaviour; fighting in public—what did he think he was doing? Spare the rod and spoil the child, my father always said, and he was right. I should have been stricter with Gil when he was a child. I've let him twist me round his little finger, that's the trouble. He has always got away with far too much, and look what it has led to! Getting the family into cheap newspapers! All my friends will be reading about it this morning!' An angry flush crept up her face, and her gnarled hand sought the beautifully carved head of a walking-stick which had once belonged to her father. The feel of its familiar shape comforted her and she sighed. 'Oh, but to lose his mother when he was only seven, poor little mite. How could I be stern with him? He cried himself to sleep every night for weeks.'

Memories flooded her mind and she stared fixedly into space for a few minutes, her eyes wide and melancholy, then her chin came up in that characteristic, defiant, determined gesture.

'All the same, he's thirty-four, too old to be brawling in nightclubs over women, having affairs, getting himself into the gossip columns, embarrassing the family. He still acts as though he were twenty. He must get married—he may think he has plenty of time, but what about me? I don't want to die without seeing Gil's children. If only I'd had more children myself. I loved my daughter deeply, but I wish I had had others, if only... Oh, what's the point of saying if only? You can't change the past by wishing. Gil must get married soon, he's put it off long enough. What's wrong with the men in this family? They all marry late, they seem afraid of marriage—or afraid of loving enough to want to marry? I've never quite known which! His grandfather waited to get married until he was nearly fifty, and then he proposed a week after I met him. I was so taken aback, but I didn't hesitate. We both knew, and we were so happy, but we hardly had a life together before he was killed in that stupid accident. If we had had a few more years, I might have managed to have other children. Jumping fences at his age! Sheer arrogant folly! I couldn't have borne to live with any other man, any more than George ever married again after my poor little Christina died. Everyone said he married her for the Westbrook money, but it wasn't true. He loved her, it broke his heart when she died, and it will break my heart if Gil doesn't get married before I die. I am going to have to take drastic measures, I can see that. I must scare him into getting married.'

She lifted the walking-stick and banged on the floor with it in a peremptory way. A moment later the door opened and a woman hurried into the room, flustered and pink after climbing the narrow stairs in the high Victorian house.

'Susan, my coat,' Lady Westbrook said. 'I am going out.'

'Oh, goodness,' gasped her companion, a woman of fifty or so with wiry gingery hair and hazel eyes. 'Where are we going?'

'I am going to the store, to see my grandson, and shut your mouth, Susan. You look like a fish.'

Spring was late that year. The weather had been wet and chilly for weeks; people made their hurried, frowning way to work in London's crowded streets hunched under umbrellas in the drizzling rain, or gloomily contemplated the weather from indoors, wishing they did not have to go out.

Most people were still wearing winter clothes. That morning, Caroline was wearing a full-skirted apricot wool dress which gave a little warmth to her very ordinary brown hair and grey eyes, and gave a glow to her olive skin. She was not a pretty girl; her features were unmemorable, although not ugly, but she had a certain style of her own; she knew what suited her and what didn't, her figure was quite good, slim and long-legged, with firm, rounded breasts, and she had learnt to look confident, which helped to hide the scars of uncertainty left on her when she was younger by some bad experiences of men on the make.

The trouble was, her father was a very wealthy man; he had inherited a chain of department stores in the north of England and had built on that foundation until today he was even buying stores across Europe and in America. He was a man of enormous energy—he had to keep moving, never satisfied, constantly adding to his empire, growing richer every day. Caroline was his only child; one day she would inherit everything he owned, and that made her a target for every man who thought marrying money was the easy way to get rich.

When she joined her father at the breakfast table he eyed her with fond pride. 'You look very pretty—new dress? It suits you.'

Caro smiled at him without saying that she had had the dress for a year. Fred Ramsgate never remembered her clothes, although he was always complimenting her on them. His love for her made him blind to how plain she was, and it was comforting to know he thought she was pretty, but it could be embarrassing when he talked to other people as if she were one of the seven wonders of the world. It always made her want to fall through the floor. She hated to see the hidden smiles, the secret amusement in men's eyes, as they listened and pretended to agree. Ever since she was a girl she had found it humiliating, but she loved her father too much to tell him frankly how she felt. He wouldn't understand; he would be baffled and hurt.

'Going somewhere special?' Fred asked her as she poured herself coffee, and she wished he wouldn't give her that hopeful look. Ever since she'd left school he had been waiting for her to get married, and questioning her eagerly about any men she met.

That wouldn't have been so bad if he hadn't been over-eager to find her a husband, constantly inviting eligible bachelors to dinner and spending the evening telling them what a wonderful wife Caroline would make while she squirmed in her chair, and glared blackly at the unfortunate male getting her father's sales talk. Even if she did like one of the men she had to freeze him off, and it was much worse when the man pretended to be enthralled, because while her father could not see through such pretences, she could—but how could she say anything when it was his love for her that made him act that way?

'Have you got a date?' he asked, and she drily told him,

'I'm having lunch with Amy.'

'Amy, eh?' Fred Ramsgate repeated, smiling broadly. He had a soft spot for Caroline's old schoolfriend, who was breathlessly feminine when in the presence of any member of the opposite sex. A pocket Venus, under five feet high, Amy had a pretty, rounded figure, blonde hair, big blue eyes, dimples in her chin, and a soft, sweet voice. One look at her and most men wanted to protect her. In fact, Amy was acting; she was no leftover from the Victorian era, she was a saleswoman, a good one, with a tough, commercial mind, and she earned an excellent salary in a London fashion house. Men couldn't see past her looks, though; they fell over themselves to make dates with her.

Maybe I should try acting weak and helpless? Caro had often thought wryly. It was a great technique, but it was not one she had ever managed to acquire. She had always been too angry to pretend to be sweet.

'Where are you eating?' asked Fred, shaking out his morning paper and glancing at the front page.

'Westbrooks,' said Caro, spreading marmalade on her wholemeal toast.

Her father gave a yelp, his eyes riveted on the newspaper. 'What?'

'Westbrooks,' Caro said, puzzled by his expression. 'You're still targeting it, aren't you? You haven't given up since Lady Westbrook turned your last offer down?'

'You know I never give up when I really want something,' Fred said complacently, proud of his own obstinacy.

'You're a bulldog,' Caro agreed, perfectly under-standing his smug satisfaction, and affectionately amused by it. Making a target of yet another store and working out ways and means of acquiring it, often in the face of furious opposition, kept Fred's adrenalin going, made him happy, and she approved of that, approved of any-thing that made her father happy. Secretly, though, she couldn't understand why he felt the need to add yet more possessions to the ones he already owned but then she had not been poor as a child. Fred had; his father had begun as a poorly paid shop assistant and it was not until Fred had been in his late teens that the Ramsgate family fortunes had begun to rise. The scars of that early poverty remained and were undoubtedly the mainspring of his drive to success.

Fred had a look in his eye that she recognised, a dreamy, yet determined look. 'Westbrooks is special, Caro. You're too young, you wouldn't know what Westbrooks meant, years ago, when I was a lad. It had glamour and style, like a Fred Astaire-Ginger Rogers film. Life was pretty grey on the whole, and when you walked into Westbrooks you were in another world. Anyone who was anybody shopped there, all the bright young things of the twenties and thirties. I can re-member seeing it all lit up for Christmas on my first trip to London. Pure magic. I never dreamt of owning it then, of course. Might as well have dreamt of owning the moon.'

'Isn't that still true?' Caro asked gently. 'That family will never sell, surely? They're financially sound, aren't they?'

'Unfortunately,' Fred said wryly, grimacing.

'And Gilham Martell is doing a good job running the place, you told me.'

Fred nodded. 'He's modernised it since he took over—a pity I didn't move my operation south before his father died. The store was very undervalued then; no changes had been made for years and it was way behind the times. The shares were well below their real value. But since Martell took over the store has begun to make a handsome profit, and shares have shot up. They're in such a great position—a marvellous site, right there in Oxford Street. I've been looking for somewhere in that part of London ever since we made the move down here.'

'That's why Amy and I eat there every so often. I know you're still interested in the store, and I keep an eye on the way things are going there.' Caro visited other stores in the same way and for the same reason; Fred's ambitions were widespread.

Fred gave her an approving look. 'Good girl. I'm not giving up on Westbrooks; it is just what we need—a flagship, or do I mean a symbol? To tell the world we've arrived.'

'I think they know that, Dad!' Caro was second in command in the accounts department of their London office; she was very well aware of the firm's financial standing. 'Do we really need any symbol or flagship? We have our logo and our name. And if Lady Westbrook doesn't want to sell—and she is the major shareholder with that fifty-one per cent of the shares—what chance have you got of ever getting control of the store?'

'You never know, life's always full of surprises.' Fred started laughing again. 'Even for the high and mighty Westbrooks!'

Baffled, Caro said, 'I wish you'd share the joke, whatever it is!'

Fred laid his newspaper on the table and stabbed a thick finger down at the photograph dominating the front page. 'That's the joke, and it isn't going to be a pleasant one for Lady Westbrook. I can imagine how the old lady is going to react to it! I'm told she hates scandal and gossip about her family, so she certainly isn't going to like this.'

Caro stared at the tough dark face in the picture, pursed her lips and whistled before reading the text beside the photograph. 'So that's Gil Martell. He must have quite a temper. I wouldn't like to meet him on a dark night!'

Or would I? she thought, taking a second look. He was just the type she hated—arrogantly sure of himself, sexy and far too aware of it, a man used to pushing others around, but... She had another look and reluctantly had to admit that there was something about him, something about his lustrous dark eyes, in the curl of his lip, the jut of his jaw... She wouldn't say she found him attractive exactly, yet she knew she would always have to give him a second look.

'Handsome fellow, isn't he?' said her father, also considering that face.

Caro shrugged. 'I suppose so. If you like the type.'

'You don't?' Her father watched her narrowly. 'Other women seem to like Martell. This isn't the first time he's got into trouble over a woman, after all. I don't read the gossip columns myself, but I'm told he's regularly in them; there's always talk of him and some new woman. I don't suppose his grandmother likes that much, either. He's too old for that sort of thing—he ought to get married and stop having fun.'

'Can I quote you on that, Dad?' Caro asked, laughing, then glanced at her watch and got hurriedly to her feet. 'I must go, or I'll be late for work.' She might be the chairman's daughter, but she was treated just like any other employee. She had to be at her desk by nine, and from the first day at work she had made sure of being punctual, working hard, never clock-watching. In fact, she worked harder than most people did, often staying late, working hours of unpaid overtime, merely because she had got absorbed in what she was doing, or knew that it had to be finished that evening and could not wait until the next day. She had got her promotion because she deserved it and had worked for it, not because she was next in line to run the entire company.

Fred looked at his own watch. He usually got to work early too, but today he was visiting several of his London stores and was not going to the office until later. 'See you at the finance committee meeting, this afternoon,' he said, as Caro made for the door.

'Three o'clock,' she agreed, giving him a wave as she vanished.

It was a busy morning for her. The accounts department had put together the usual monthly financial report for study by the finance committee, but there were several late additions which had to be circulated so that members of the committee could study them, and Caro hardly had time to think before noon, when she broke for lunch.

Although Caro was only the second in command she did most of the organisational and daily work. It was a vital job in the company: she monitored salaries and costs, planned the company's annual budget, examined expenditure in detail and authorised payments. The head of the department was fifty-nine years old and a mere cypher; he was working out his last year without enthusiasm. He would retire at sixty, collect a pension and move into the country, leaving Caro in charge in name as well as in fact.

Of course, some people sneered about that, and whispered behind her back or openly hinted that she was getting such power simply because of who she was, but although her progress had been swifter than normal, and probably there were others who could do her work as well as she did, Caro had no doubts about taking promotion, or about her own capacity. She knew she had brains, she could do the job and do it well, and she worked hard. If she hadn't been very good, Fred would never have promoted her. He was a ruthless realist where his precious company was concerned, and so was Caro. She would one day, she hoped, run the company, and, meanwhile, she wasn't going to apologise or feel guilty about being her father's daughter.

Amy was waiting at their table when Caro arrived at the Penthouse Restaurant on the top floor of Westbrooks. 'You're always late!' she complained as Caro dropped into the seat opposite her. 'As you're the boss's daughter I would have thought you could slip out when you liked!'

'That's just why I can't,' Caro said, picking up the menu as the waitress approached. 'Have you ordered? Good, then I'll just have melon and the bean and pasta salad.'

'Pasta? So fattening, don't do it!'

Caro laughed. 'Pasta's OK if there's no rich sauce with it. Shall we have wine? No? Oh, well, mineral water for me, too.' When the waitress had gone, she said, 'I'm sorry I was late, Amy—I got stuck in traffic. London is hell these days.'

'So is life,' Amy said mournfully.

Caro gave her an amused look. 'Is it? What's happened now?' Amy's life was full of dramas; it kept Caro constantly entertained.

'Johnny didn't go to Paris with his aunt! He took his secretary. He says it was business, but in that case why lie to me about it?'

'They always do,' said Caro drily.

'I thought Johnny was different!' Amy mourned, lip trembling.

'None of them are! They all cheat, if they can.'

'You're so cynical,' Amy accused. 'You always think the worst. You know what I think? You're still carrying a torch for Damian Shaw!'

Caro flushed angrily. 'You're out of your mind!'

Amy looked knowing. 'If I'm wrong, why have you gone red?'

'With temper!' said Caro sharply, then bit her lip as the waitress brought their first course.

She had been twenty-one when she'd got involved with Damian Shaw, a clever and charming young lawyer, and she was twenty-six now, but although she was over the pain of that affair, the anger she felt whenever she remembered it remained. Damian Shaw had humiliated her, made her fall in love with him while he was only pretending to care about her. All he had really cared about was her father's fortune. He had wounded her pride, as well as her heart. No man since had ever been given the chance.

'The only thing I'm carrying for Damian Shaw is a harpoon,' she said, forking a piece of melon, looking down. Out of the corner of her eye she noticed the newspaper Amy had been reading while she'd waited and, before Amy had the chance to say anything else about Damian, Caro asked, 'Were you reading about Gilham Martell's fight with the Earl of Jurby? I wonder if a divorce is in the offing?'

Distracted, Amy said, 'Yes, isn't it a scream? I wish I'd been there. You know him, don't you? What's he like?'

'Who?' asked Caro blankly.

'Gil Martell.'

'I've never met him—what made you think I knew him?'

'Well, we eat at Westbrooks a lot because your father wants to buy it!'

'Ssh...' Caro said in a hurry, glancing around.

'I just thought you must know the managing director of the store,' said Amy blithely.

'Amy!' spat Caro. 'Shut up. We don't talk about business, remember?' Amy was very indiscreet; she didn't seem to understand why Caro wanted to be incognito when she visited a store her father was targeting. 'I've explained about keeping a project under wraps until it's time to...'

'Pounce,' said Amy, giggling.

'I wouldn't put it quite like that,' Caro said sharply. 'I'd have said until we were ready to show our hand.'

Amy's attention wandered as a woman in a mink hat and jacket sauntered past. 'Look—that's one of ours. Perfectly matched skins; see the smooth fan style? Gorgeous, isn't it?'

'I never wear real furs,' Caro said flatly.

'Oh, but mink aren't an endangered species!' protested Amy.

'That's no reason for killing them for their fur,' said Caro, and they got bogged down in an argument they had had many times before.

The waitress whisked their plates away and was back a moment later with their main courses.

'OK, then, what about sheep?' Amy triumphantly asked. 'I'm wearing this cream wool suit…but you don't seem bothered by that.'

'They didn't have to kill the sheep, just cut its fleece, and it was probably relieved as it's summer when they do it!' Caro glanced over the suit. 'And I bet that looks better on you than it ever did on the sheep!'

Amy giggled. 'Well, I should hope so! It is gorgeous, isn't it? I got it at cost, and I bought a black dress, too…' She began to talk clothes and Caro listened wryly, not sharing Amy's obsession with fashion. She didn't share Amy's other obsession, either: with men, who always broke her heart. Fortunately, her heart mended quickly and Amy went on to a new man, a new heartbreak. Caro was not that resilient or forgetful; she had had her heart broken once and that was enough. At least I don't make the same mistake over and over again, she thought, as she and Amy said goodbye. After Damian, I've taken care never to fall in love with anyone else.

'See you next Wednesday at the Portland Club House, and then it's my treat,' said Amy, poised for flight. 'I must rush. Thanks for the lunch. Bye.'

By next week, she'll be madly in love with someone new, Caro thought, but what does her love mean when it's given and forgotten so easily? I've no intention of falling in love until I'm sure the guy is in love with me, and means it.

She took the escalators down to check on the various floors, walking slowly around, her sharp, observant eyes moving like lightning, looking out for clever arrangements, new ideas, what was selling, what wasn't. She was in the jewellery department when a man bumped into her with some force. Caro almost fell over, stumbling back against a counter. When she recovered, she turned to make some terse comment, but the man had already vanished into the lift.

It was getting late now though, and she ought to get back for the committee meeting, so she headed for the lift herself, walking fast.

'Excuse me, madam,' a man said beside her, touching her arm. 'I would like a word, if you please.'

Caro gave him a brief glance. He was middle-aged, solidly built, with eyes like chisels.

'I'm sorry, I'm in a hurry,' she said impatiently, not wanting to waste time on a sales pitch from one of the Westbrooks staff. 'Whatever you're selling, I don't want it.' And she quickened her step.

'Oh, no, you don't!' growled the stranger, clamping a hand down, hard, on her shoulder.

Startled, Caro said, 'Let go of me!' She tried to pull free, but that grip, though light, was unbreakable.

'I'm the store detective,' the big man said in his grating voice. 'We've been watching you on the monitors for the past twenty minutes loitering about, waiting for your chance to do a snatch. We've got it all on film, so don't bother to lie, and we tagged your accomplice too. He won't have got out of the store, don't hope for that. He'll be on his way to the manager's office by now, and he won't have had a chance of switching the stuff to someone else from your gang because we'll have been watching him on the monitor, wherever he went!'

'You've got the wrong person! You're making a mistake!' Caro protested.

'Just come with me, will you, madam?' the detective merely said.

She struggled angrily. 'Let go of me, you're hurting!'

'Let go of you so that you can bolt for it? I don't think so!' he said.

A little crowd, meanwhile, had gathered, staring. Caro knew she had turned dark red, and she was very tense. From the expression on the faces around her she realised she must look guilty.

'You don't want a scene in public, do you, madam?' asked the detective and, of course, she didn't. He read the look she gave him and smiled, not very pleasantly. Caro did not like him at all, but she had no choice. She had to let him steer her towards the lift.

Once in the lift the man jabbed the button with one hand while he still held her upper arm with the other. As they shot upwards, she pulled herself free, glaring at him while she massaged her arm.

'Being a store detective doesn't give you the right to push customers around. I shall complain to your boss when I see him.'

'If I hadn't insisted that you come with me, would you have come?' he asked her coolly.

'Certainly,' she said. 'If you had asked me politely!'

He laughed. 'Oh, I bet!'

The lift door opened; he propelled her out and along a wide corridor, through a mahogany door into a spacious, discreetly furnished office. A smartly dressed woman sat behind a desk, a telephone in her hand. She gave Caro a cold stare.

'Go straight in,' she said to the store detective. 'The man's in custody. Harry had no trouble with him. There was nothing on him, though; she must have the necklace. I'm just ringing down for Stella to come and strip-search her. The two of them must have been working alone, there doesn't seem to be anyone else.'

'Then he must have been passing it to her—I saw them pull the old trick of knocking into each other. I thought she'd passed it to him, but it must have been the other way round. Never mind. We've got them both.'

'You've got the wrong person!' Caro said again, and the detective grimaced at the woman behind the desk.

'We've heard that before, haven't we?'

'A hundred times!' the woman agreed, her smile contemptuous as she stared at Caro.

'This way,' the detective said to Caro. 'Sorry, I forgot. Would you kindly step this way, madam?' He gestured across the office, and she walked with him towards a door on the other side of the room. The detective knocked on the door.

A deep dark voice curtly said, 'Come in!'

Caro had just seen the name on the door. Her heart sank. Oh, no, she thought—not him! She backed like a frightened horse facing a leap into the unknown, and the detective grabbed her arm with one hand, opened the door with the other and pushed her into the room.

Caro was, by now, completely off balance. She tripped, and ended up face down on a deep-pile carpet.

'Holt! There's no need for that sort of rough stuff, especially with a woman!' the deep voice snapped.

'She tripped, sir!' the store detective hurriedly said.

Caro lifted her head, hair across her eyes, and peered wildly at a pair of highly polished black shoes, at slim, long legs in smoothly tailored dark trousers, at an immaculately cut jacket, a crisp white shirt, a dark grey silk tie, and then at a hard face. A very hard face. A face she recognised at once. Only that morning she had said she wouldn't want to meet its owner on a dark night. Well, it wasn't dark, but she still didn't want to meet Gilham Martell.

He was staring down at her as fixedly. She was glad she did not know what he was thinking. It wouldn't ever be easy to guess, she thought; he had the eyes of a poker player and the mouth of an assassin. Gilham Martell was a very nasty piece of work, almost as nasty as his store detective.

'Get up!' he ordered.

She stayed on her hands and knees, hating him. 'You're going to be sorry about this!' Her voice was shaking with rage.

He bent abruptly; a long-fingered hand fastened on her arm and yanked her to her feet, like a rag doll.

'Don't you manhandle me!' Caro yelled, pushing him away. 'This man has knocked me about, dragged me through your shop, thrown me into this room...' She was so angry she couldn't get another word out, breathing roughly.

'Holt, what the hell have you been up to?' Gilham Martell demanded, frowning.

The detective was scowling at her. 'She's exaggerating, sir! I did it by the book. I asked her to accompany me, and when she resisted I merely held her by the arm! At no time did I knock her about—she's lying.'

'You had no right to force me to come with you!' Caro threw at him. 'You made a mistake. I am not a shoplifter, and I can prove it.'

'Do so, then,' said Gilham Martell, watching her, his brows knitted.

'I'm Caroline Ramsgate,' she said, staring back at him and waiting for that to register. She saw no change in Gil Martell's face; he just waited for her to go on, and after a pause she did. 'I am Fred Ramsgate's daughter.'

His face changed then, dramatically. The dark eyes narrowed and hardened, the mouth became tight and straight, his colour darkened. After a moment he repeated, 'You're Fred Ramsgate's daughter,' in a flat voice.

'Yes,' she snapped. 'And he's going to make you wish you'd never been born.'

There was a long silence, then Gilham Martell said to the detective, 'You can go. I'll deal with this.'

The man quietly left the room. The door closed and Gil pushed her firmly down into a chair and sat down on the edge of his desk, his arms folded.

'Show me some proof of your identity,' he said in a clipped, hard tone, and Caro opened her handbag and produced her driving licence, her wallet, a handful of snapshots of herself with her father in Rome at a recent conference. Gilham Martell only needed to take a brief glance then he handed them all back to her, frowning blackly.

'The minute I set eyes on you coming through that door, I knew I was going to have trouble from you,' he said, almost to himself.

CHAPTER TWO

IT HAD been a fraught day for Gil Martell. His grandmother had visited him that morning, breathing fire and thunder, and making threats he didn't take seriously but which had left him edgy and irritable. He understood why she wanted him to get married and start a family. Occasionally he wanted that himself—but he had never met a woman he couldn't live without, and he wasn't going to settle for less. Nor was he about to pick the first girl he saw. One day he would probably marry, but she had to be right; he was looking for a special woman, a very special woman, and he hadn't found her yet. When he'd said that to his grandmother, though, she had become even angrier and shouted that if he hadn't found a girl and married her by the end of the year, she was selling the store and leaving all her money to charity.

'Do that!' he had yelled back, resenting the blackmail, and she had walked out without looking back, leaving Gil in a raging temper.

Which was why he was in no mood to be gentle with shoplifters. The store lost thousands of pounds of stock to shoplifters every year, and, added to that, it cost a fortune to employ store detectives and electronic surveillance systems. If there was anything Gil really hated, it was a shoplifter, and he didn't mean some sick woman who was having a temporary problem which came out as kleptomania, he meant criminals who made a full-time business of stealing from stores.

Every year the problem seemed to get worse; they were losing so much money that it was a nightmare and something had to be done about it.

He had stared down angrily at the girl when she first fell on the floor at his feet. She was no beauty: straight brown hair, a very ordinary face, except for those eyes he could see through the fine strands of hair which had fallen over her temples—bright, angry grey eyes which glittered at him and were far from ordinary. He had absently noted their beauty, then told himself to stop wasting his time. The girl was a thief!

And then she had dropped her bombshell, and Gil found it hard to cope with the realisation of what had happened. His store detective had accused Fred Ramsgate's daughter of being a shoplifter!

'I'll deal with this,' he had wearily told Holt, and the store detective had stared, puzzled, then slowly left the room, no doubt quite unaware what he had done. He should read the financial pages of his newspaper, thought Gil grimly.

'This is rapidly turning into one of the worst days of my life,' he said aloud.

'And it isn't over yet,' Caro said. 'May I use your phone? I want to ring my father.'

She was still holding her documents and photographs in one hand; she laid them on the desk to pick up the telephone, but before she had begun to dial the number, Gil leaned right over to stare hard at one of the snapshots and she felt colour rise in her cheeks as she glanced at it, too, and saw that it was one taken on a beach in Florida last year, showing her in a brief bikini which left nothing to the imagination. Caro knew she didn't have to be ashamed of her figure—she might not have a pretty face, but the rest of her was OK—yet for some reason it made her edgy to have Gil Martell's cold eyes assessing her half-naked body, especially when he looked up from the photo to skim a glance from her head to her feet.

'What a difference clothes make!' he drawled, his brows lifting in derision.

She didn't bother to reply, just scooped up the photo, and all the other things, and put them away, her hands not quite steady and her face hot. Damn him! What was he thinking, giving her that mocking little smile? He had the eyes of a poker player, dark wells you could drown in without ever discovering what lay behind them. She stared into those eyes, then shook herself impatiently.

'May I make my phone call now?' she asked with ice in her voice.

'There's still something I'd like explained,' Gil said, quite unaffected by her coldness. 'What were you doing, loitering about in the store? They had monitored you for quite a while before you were detained, and you were acting suspiciously, there's no doubt about that. They didn't imagine it. You weren't shopping. You didn't buy anything. You hung about on various floors, watching the staff, watching customers. What were you up to? And don't tell me you weren't up to anything because I wouldn't believe it. You were in the store for a purpose—what was it?'

'I was checking you out,' she coolly admitted.

He stared. 'Doing what?'

'Checking out the store.' Her tone was half defiant; she knew he was going to resent what she had been doing, but she wasn't lying about it.

'What does that mean, exactly?' Gil Martell asked in a dangerously quiet voice.

'I was trying to get an idea of your strengths and weaknesses on the sales floors, assess the flow of customers, the displays, the loss leaders, everything.'

'You were spying on us!' His voice held distaste and her colour deepened. He made it sound like espionage, and it was nothing of the kind. Her eyes flashed resentment at him.

'It isn't against the law to wander around a department store and assess it. Any customer could do it any time of day.'

'An ordinary customer wouldn't be planning to buy us up!'

'My reasons are irrelevant. The only question is: was I breaking the law? And the answer is no.'

'And that's the only thing that matters, is it? Staying inside the law and not getting caught?'

The words, the dry tone were meant to insult her, and she felt herself getting angrier. 'Of course not! I didn't say that, you're just twisting my words! My father has made an open bid for your store——'

'And been turned down!'

'For the moment, maybe, but things change, people change their minds.'

'We won't,' he tersely told her.

She ignored that, carrying on in a flat, cool voice. 'And in the meantime we always like to keep an eye on the current situation so that, if a property comes on to the market suddenly, we have a pretty fair idea of the state of affairs inside the store, and what it is therefore worth. On paper, something can look terrific value, but when you take a closer look you find it isn't quite such a bargain, so...'

'So your father sends you to snoop around?' he disdainfully murmured.

Caro felt like hitting him. She stared at him with dislike, but she wouldn't give him the satisfaction of letting him know how angry she was getting.

She wasn't sure why, but she did not want to betray herself to this man. She wanted to keep any emotion she felt—rage or humiliation, or pain—hidden from him, and that was puzzling in itself because she had never felt like that about any other man.

'Look, Mr Martell,' she said in a leashed voice, holding on to her temper with difficulty, 'I was in your restaurant, having lunch with a friend, and afterwards I wandered around the store to see what sort of business you were doing. I fail to see what was wrong with that, and I'm sure as hell not going to apologise for it.'

'Then you won't expect me to apologise because my security staff mistook your prowling about for the behaviour of a shoplifter!' he snapped.

'I wouldn't be so foolish as to expect common courtesy from you, Mr Martell!' she snarled back, and then they were both silent, staring at each other because their raised voices reverberated in the office and startled them both.

Caro had to do something to break that silence; she lifted her wrist and stared blankly at her watch. 'I have to go,' she said in a flat voice. 'I won't bother to make that call. I'm expected at an important meeting at three o'clock and it's half-past two now. I'll see my father there and fill him in on all this. You can expect to hear from our lawyers.'

As she turned to go, Gil Martell caught hold of her arm and she jumped what felt like six feet into the air, her whole body tensing as if she had had an electric shock.

She looked at the hand on her sleeve and then up into his frowning face. 'Will you take your hand off me?'

she almost whispered. 'I've had enough of being man-handled this afternoon.'

His hand fell; he pushed both hands into his pockets in a deliberate way, eyeing her with hostility. 'When you said you were Fred Ramsgate's daughter I couldn't believe it for a minute. I hadn't supposed Ramsgate had ever done anything so human as get himself a daughter. But I can see the resemblance now. Very much so.'

'Good!' she snapped. 'I'm glad!' She knew he hadn't meant it as a compliment, but she insisted on taking it as one.

Gil ignored the interruption. He talked on coldly, staring down at her out of those night-black eyes. 'Your father doesn't believe in ethics, any more than you do—he hasn't built his empire up, he's snatched it from other men, men who worked all their lives to build a strong business only to have your father come out of nowhere to grab it from them. He has clawed his way to the top using the tactics of the jungle, and clearly you're a credit to him.'

Caro was hurt and bitterly angry at the same time. Hoarsely, she spat back, 'I hope I do take after my father, in every way, so you can take that look off your face. I love my father, he's a great man, and I'm proud of being his daughter.'

She walked to the door, half expecting him to try to stop her leaving, and hoping he would so that she could have the satisfaction of slapping his face, but he just sat there on the edge of his desk, and did nothing at all but swing those long, athletic legs of his, watching her walk out of his office and slam the door behind her.

Caro got a taxi back to the head office of Rams Stores Ltd and went straight up to her father's office, to catch him before he left for the finance committee meeting.

He was going to be furious about what had happened, and she disliked making him angry; but she couldn't keep it a secret, because it might still have unpleasant repercussions. If the Press got hold of the story it would be embarrassing, for one thing; which was one very strong reason for taking legal action against Gil Martell. That way she would be covering herself. If she didn't sue it might look as if she could be guilty of shoplifting.

Her father was at his desk running an eye over the various reports which were to be discussed that afternoon in the committee. He looked up with an abstracted smile, surprise in his eyes, as she walked in.

'Hello, darling. Nice lunch with Amy?' he said, and then his gaze sharpened and he said anxiously, 'What's wrong, Caro?' getting to his feet at once.

She hadn't meant to burst into tears; she had thought she was just angry, and she hadn't realised until that moment just how upset she was, but as her father put an arm around her the tears sprang into her eyes.

'Darling, whatever's happened?' Fred asked, hugging her.

She dried her eyes with a stifled sob, took a deep breath and told him, and after a while he held her away from him, his big hands gripping her arms, staring down into her flushed face incredulously.

'You were accused of being a shoplifter?'

She wasn't surprised that he should be so staggered. At the time she had been too stunned and horrified to realise exactly what was happening to her, and later, in Gil Martell's office, she had been so angry that adrenalin had carried her along, but now that it was all over her legs had turned to jelly and at the same time she couldn't believe she had actually been treated like that.

'They accused me of stealing,' she shakily repeated, nodding vehemently. 'Right in the store, with hundreds of people watching, and the detective wouldn't listen to a word I said—he made me go up to Gil Martell's office, and threw me across——'

'Threw you?' roared Fred Ramsgate, going purple around the neck.

'Well, pushed me,' she said, reluctantly telling the truth. 'He pushed me into the office and I tripped and fell . . . face down on the carpet.'

'Face down?' Fred seemed to be having difficulty breathing.

'I was so humiliated!' Caro wailed, tears of rage in her eyes, although it was Gil Martell's comments on her father that were upsetting her, not the way she herself had been treated. Gil Martell had said such vicious things about her father. They were all lies, and she hated him.

'I'll kill him,' Fred said. 'When I get hold of him, he'll wish he'd never been born.'

'He dragged me up and shook me——'

'This detective?'

'Gil Martell.'

'Martell himself? I'll kill him, I'll kill both of them,' her father repeated, breathing like a bellows.

'And interrogated me, as if I were a criminal!' Caro said, remembering.

'I'll interrogate him!' Fred snarled.

'He bullied me! If you'd heard the way he talked to me!'

'I'll bully him!' Fred promised, his face grim and tight.

Caro was beginning to calm down and feel much better, now that she had been able to talk about the experience, let out some of the nervous tension that had built up inside her. Her father was always on her side, ready to spring to her defence, as he had throughout her life, and she loved him for it, but his rage worried her; she was always afraid he might have a heart attack in one of his tempers, and she gave him an uncertain look, biting her lip. Fred watched her, frowning.

'What else? Are you keeping something back? Tell me, Caro, I want to know everything that happened. Why are you looking like that?'

'Nothing else happened! But I don't want you to waste your time on Gilham Martell. Let our lawyers deal with him.'

The intercom on his desk buzzed—he scowled, and jabbed a finger down on a button, barking, 'I'm busy.'

His secretary's quiet voice said, 'Lady Westbrook on the line for you, sir.'

Fred Ramsgate's face altered. 'Lady Westbrook?' He glanced at Caro, his mouth wry. 'She's heard, and she's ringing to apologise—what's the betting? What a family! They embarrass my daughter and knock her about, then think they can talk me out of suing, and Martell doesn't even ring me himself, he gets his grandmother to do it! I've a good mind not to talk to her. They needn't think they can sweet talk us out of suing them!'

'I hate Gil Martell,' Caro said fiercely, saw her father's startled face and swallowed. She didn't want to arouse any curiosity about her feelings towards Gil Martell. Hurriedly, she added, 'But maybe you should talk to Lady Westbrook?' Why had Gil's grandmother rung, anyway? 'I'm curious about what she's going to say— aren't you?' she added lightly, smiling at her father.

'I suppose so,' Fred admitted, grimacing. 'And it will be a pleasure to hear that old dragon-lady having to eat humble pie!' He brusquely told his secretary to put the call through.

'Good afternoon, Mr Ramsgate,' a sharp, yet manifestly old voice said a few seconds later.

'Afternoon, Lady Westbrook,' Fred grunted.

'How are you?'

'Well enough; how are you?' Fred asked in that surly tone.

'I am well, thank you.' Lady Westbrook paused and Caro waited tensely for whatever she was about to say, but instead of mentioning the incident at the department store that afternoon, the old lady said, 'Mr Ramsgate, I am ringing to invite you to dinner.'

'Dinner?' Fred repeated, looking taken aback. 'You're inviting us to dinner?'

'Us?' Lady Westbrook sounded puzzled. 'Oh, of course, you mean your wife.'

'My wife's been dead for years,' Fred said flatly. 'I meant Caro—my daughter. You'll want her to be there. This concerns her, too, remember.'

'Oh?' Lady Westbrook sounded unsure about that, and Fred's brows met.

'Of course it does!' he said in a rough voice. 'Think of us as one person, Lady Westbrook. She isn't just my daughter, she's also my right hand. One day she'll take over from me, and we're very close, both as father and daughter, and as business partners. What matters to me, matters to her—and vice versa.'

'Oh, I see,' said the old lady, her voice clearing. 'I understand.'

Caro hoped she did; she hoped Lady Westbrook now realised just what her grandson had done when he'd insulted and humiliated Fred Ramsgate's daughter.

'Then I shall be happy to see you both at dinner,' Lady Westbrook said. Caro wondered what she looked like— her autocratic, assured tone was very reminiscent of the way her grandson talked and looked. 'Now, how soon can you come? The sooner, the better, I think, don't you?'

'I agree,' Fred muttered.

'Have you your diary there? This is very short notice—but I suppose you aren't free tonight?'

'Tonight?' Fred glanced down at his leatherbound diary, which lay open on the desk, then looked up at Caro, silently questioning her. She nodded agreement and her father said into the phone, 'No, we aren't doing anything tonight.'

'Then will you both come to dinner? Seven-thirty for eight?'

'Seven-thirty,' said Fred in a faintly breathless voice. 'Yes, we'll be there.'

'Do you know Regents Park?'

'I live there, so I ought to.'

'Really? I didn't know that. I'm in Marlborough Crescent, number one. Are you familiar with the road?'

'We're just around the corner from you.' Fred mentioned their address and Lady Westbrook laughed.

'Oh, I know the house. You have a wonderful magnolia tree in the centre of your front lawns; I always admire it when I drive past.'

Fred couldn't help smiling at that; his magnolia was his pride and joy.

'Well, then, I will see you at seven-thirty.' The phone clicked and Lady Westbrook was gone.

Fred slowly replaced his receiver, his expression almost incredulous. 'I don't believe she's invited us to dinner—she wouldn't even speak to me when I made the offer for the store. Her lawyers dealt with the whole thing. She refused to meet me, didn't acknowledge my letters.

I gather she's an autocratic old lady, and probably a snob. I was given the impression she despised me as a self-made man, *nouveau riche*, vulgar. She has never worked in the store, of course; she didn't start at the bottom, like me, or have to learn the business. She's a lady, and she owns it without knowing anything about how it is run. She has always left that to the men—her husband, her son, and now her grandson. I didn't meet him; I didn't even meet her lawyers, come to that. They didn't discuss the matter so much as just say no, and then refused to talk any more. They made it clear that I was getting the brush-off. They couldn't even be bothered to meet me, I wasn't important enough, they practically laughed at me for daring to make an offer. And now she's asking me to dinner. I don't believe it.'

'They must be very scared,' Caro said, thinking of Gil Martell with angry satisfaction. Would he be there tonight? Maybe his grandmother would make him apologise to her? He would hate it if she did! Caro hardly knew him, but already she realised that Gil Martell had more than his fair share of pride, not to mention an inflated idea of his own self-importance. Well, she wanted to see him climb down from that pinnacle he thought he lived on—climb down and go on his knees to her! Nothing less would salve her own humiliation over being thrown at his feet like a slave-girl flung down in front of her new owner.

'I wish I had time to buy a new dress!' she thought aloud and her father laughed.

'As if you need one! You have wardrobes full of lovely things!' He got to his feet, looking at his watch in consternation. 'Time to go—it's just three o'clock and we're going to be late for the meeting. Now, where the devil are those reports?'

Caro, for once, found it hard to concentrate on work that afternoon. Her mind was occupied elsewhere and she had to keep dragging her attention back to the matter in hand, aware of her father's concerned glances, the puzzled expressions of the other members of the committee.

She was glad to get away from the office at six o'clock, and when she got home went straight upstairs. After all, she only had an hour in which to get ready to see Gil Martell again, and there was a lot to do!

Fred was always punctual; he had learnt to live by the clock at a very early age and old habits died hard. Whatever the pressure of business, he made sure he was on time for appointments, and at seven-thirty precisely he and Caro were on the doorstep of Lady Westbrook's beautiful house, ringing the doorbell and, while they waited for the door to open, gazing with admiration at the elegant cream façade.

'It's a huge place for one old woman to live in,' Fred murmured in a low voice.

'Maybe her grandson lives here too?' Caro's nerves were jumping like grasshoppers and she was breathless. She didn't know if she was up to facing Gil Martell across a dinner table, and swapping polite small talk with him.

She stiffened as the front door opened. A short, stout woman in a neat grey dress greeted them politely, took their coats and showed them into the drawing-room, where Lady Westbrook was waiting. Caro merely got a brief impression of a high-ceilinged hall, glossy with panelling and highly polished parquet, then she was watching the old woman rising from a straight-backed Victorian armchair.

Lady Westbrook was oddly familiar to her; for a second Caro was thrown by the resemblance to Gil Martell—those dark eyes, the long nose and autocratic air all looked somehow different on a woman, especially such an old one.

There were obvious differences, other than that: her hair must have been black at one time but was now totally white, as fine as spun silk around her spare-boned face. Her skin was wrinkled and her body seemed almost fleshless—yet, as she came forward with a smile to shake hands with Fred Ramsgate, she moved with unmistakable grace and her face held charm. Fred visibly responded, his own face softening. He was very susceptible to charm in a woman of any age, from two to a hundred!

'This is my daughter Caroline,' Fred introduced, and the two women shook hands, exchanging glances.

'And so you work with your father? Do you find that interesting?' Lady Westbrook seemed incredulous, and Caro laughed shortly.

'Very, I enjoy my work. I'm a qualified accountant, and did a course at a business school when I left school.'

'Women's lives have changed so much since I was young!' Lady Westbrook said, and Caro wondered if she envied her, or disapproved. 'Do sit down, my dear, sit here, near me. My eyesight isn't as good as it was, and I like to be able to see my guests. Now, what would you both like to drink? A dry sherry or a sweet one?'

The housekeeper poured them all sherry and vanished, and Lady Westbrook delicately sipped from her glass, then turned her commanding dark eyes upon Fred.

'We do not want to ruin our meal by talking business, do we, so shall we get it out of the way beforehand?'

Caro's face tightened; she and her father exchanged looks. 'As you wish,' Fred said flatly.

Lady Westbrook studied him, her face expressionless. 'I am, of course, presuming that you are still interested?'

'Still interested?' he repeated, and she nodded.

'In buying Westbrooks.'

Caro sat up, almost spilling her sherry. Fred's mouth dropped open. Whatever he had been expecting it had not been that, but he hurriedly pulled himself together.

'Yes, yes, of course, very interested.'

'Very well, then, tomorrow I will instruct my people to open negotiations with you,' Lady Westbrook said, and at that instant the door was flung open with a crash and Gil Martell appeared, his face dark with rage.

Caro's nerves leapt violently, as if at the touch of fire. She had wondered if he was going to be there, and how he would look at her. Well, now she knew. He was in a nasty temper again—was that his usual mood or was it only when he saw her? He glared across the room at her and her father, and then threw a furious look at his grandmother.

'What the hell is going on here?'

'I do not recall inviting you to dinner, Gilham,' Lady Westbrook icily said. 'You are forgetting your manners. Don't you see that I have guests? Let me introduce you— this is Mr Ramsgate and his daughter Caroline——'

'I know who they are,' Gil snarled. 'What I want to know is what are they doing here?'

'I invited them to dine with me.' Lady Westbrook was rigid with offence, a spot of dark red in each withered cheek.

'Why?' demanded Gil through his teeth, and his grandmother coldly answered him, drawing herself up in her chair.

'I don't have to explain myself to you, Gilham, but if you really must know, I am discussing selling Westbrooks to Mr Ramsgate.'

Gil Martell's teeth met and dark red surged up his face. 'Over my dead body!'

CHAPTER THREE

'GLADLY,' Caro jumped in, unable to resist the temptation, and Lady Westbrook looked at her in astonishment, as if she had never heard anyone talk to her grandson like that, then she began to laugh. Gil wasn't either so surprised or so amused. He had met Caroline Ramsgate before.

'You keep out of this!' he told her with dislike.

'You deserved that, Gilham, and don't be rude to Miss Ramsgate!' Lady Westbrook said, stifling her laughter. 'And will you kindly leave? I didn't invite you to join us.'

'Because you knew I would never agree to selling the store!'

'Your agreement is not necessary, fortunately. I own the majority of the shares.'

'You haven't even consulted the board!'

'I don't need to consult anyone. The shares belong to me. If I choose to sell them, that's my business. And you can't say I didn't tell you my intentions, because I told you this morning that I had made up my mind to sell the shares. If you didn't believe I meant it, that is not my fault. I made myself quite clear, surely! I have never suffered from an inability to express myself with clarity.'

Thickly, Gil Martell said, 'For heaven's sake, think! You know what it will mean! Whoever owns those shares controls the firm—you can't seriously want Westbrooks to go out of the family! It's crazy! Just because you're angry with me over some stupid little——' He broke off, remembering that Caro and her father were there, threw them a brief, angry look, his flush deepening, and muttered in an offhand voice, 'Look, I want to talk to my grandmother alone—would you mind leaving? This is a private matter, a family matter.'

Fred Ramsgate mumbled, 'Of course...' and got up to go, and Caro rose as well, rather reluctantly, since she had been fascinated by the argument which had been raging. It was very revealing and explained a lot about Gil Martell. He obviously loved his grandmother; she had brought him up when his mother died, and they must be very close—but did he resent her domination, too?

After all, she owned the shares which controlled the company, yet Gil had been managing the store for quite a time now, always subject to his grandmother's will, constantly reminded to whom the power finally belonged. He was not the sort of man to like that situation. He was far too arrogant and assertive.

As Caro moved, her full-skirted tawny skirts rustled, brushing her slim legs. She loved the dress she had chosen to wear; it came from her favourite English designer. Made of taffeta, it was the colour of good sherry, the style a modern version of an Edwardian dress, with a high neck, a smooth-fitting bodice which emphasised her rounded breasts, a tight little waist and long, full skirts beneath which were hidden layers of crisp lacy petticoats. It made her feel very feminine.

Gil Martell watched her, his gleaming eyes briefly flicking up and down her body with an assessment that made her skin hot. It wasn't that she felt he was attracted to her, only that he was the sort of man who always noticed women, was aware of their sexuality even if he disliked them.

Caro understood that because she didn't like Gil Martell, either, yet she couldn't help being very conscious of his masculinity. All the same, she prickled under his gaze.

'How dare you ask my guests to leave?' flared Lady Westbrook. 'Sit down again, Mr Ramsgate, take no notice of my grandson.'

'We can't talk about this in front of strangers!' Gil bit out.

'This is no time and place to discuss the matter at all,' his grandmother said. 'I am giving a dinner party, not conducting a business meeting. I merely asked Mr Ramsgate if he was still interested in buying the store, and he says that he is, so we can start having talks with him.'

'We?' retorted Gil. 'I have no intention of having talks with him—or anyone who wants to buy my store.'

'Your store?' the old lady repeated coldly, her eyes remote. 'You are forgetting—it is my store, Gilham. That is something you have overlooked all along. I own the store, and I can do what I like with it. It is time you realised that. I employ you to run it for me, you earn a very good salary for doing so, too, but you do not own it, nor will you be a party to the take-over discussions. If I decide to sell, Mr Ramsgate will be negotiating with my lawyers.'

'If?' He seized on the word like a cat on the tail of a vanishing mouse. 'So you haven't actually made up your mind yet?'

She shrugged. 'I am investigating the possibilities, let us say, of selling to Mr Ramsgate. My lawyers will handle it at first, since I dislike getting involved in business dealings, but I will make the final decision, and before I do, I promise, I will consult you, although I can't promise to accept your advice. You will have your chance to say what you think, though. Now, I won't have you ruining my dinner party. These are my guests, and you are embarrassing them. Would you please leave?'

For a second he didn't move, his long, athletic body so taut Caro felt she could see the tension in the muscles and nerves. A little tic pulsed in his throat, just below his ear, and his dark eyes glittered like polished jet.

She waited, expecting another harsh outburst, but suddenly he swung on his heel and strode to the door, only to pull up and stand there for a moment, his back to them, his head lowered as if he was having a struggle with himself. At last he took an audible, long, deep breath, swung round and gave his grandmother a rueful and charming smile. Caro could see the little boy in it, the coaxing, butter-wouldn't-melt-in-his-mouth little boy who had always been able to get round his grandmother with that smile.

'I'm sorry, Grandmother,' he said softly. 'I lost my temper again. I didn't want to do that, I didn't mean to—I'd come round to apologise for the argument we had this morning, but it was such a shock to find you had already got a buyer lined up that I got angry all over again. I'm sorry.'

Lady Westbrook gave him a cool stare, her mouth indenting. 'It's time you learnt to handle that temper of yours, Gilham. And don't you think you owe my guests an apology, too? They didn't come here tonight expecting a scene like that.'

He walked back towards them, holding that charming expression on his face, although Caro could see the betraying glitter of his dark eyes all the time and she knew he was acting. He held out his hand, smiling with deceptive warmth. 'Mr Ramsgate, I beg your pardon, please forget my bad manners.'

Fred looked at the hand, but did not take it. Instead, he said, 'Mr Martell, this morning my daughter was treated very badly in your store.'

'That was a stupid mistake, for which I assure you I apologised,' Gil said smoothly, letting his hand drop.

'That's all very well,' said Fred. 'Words are cheap enough, aren't they? You say it was a mistake—maybe, but even if it was a mistake, why did your store detective treat Caro so roughly? She says she was thrown across a room, dragged about, shaken...'

Gil Martell grimaced. 'The man in question has been fired. He didn't act that way on my instructions, I assure you. Of course it was completely contrary to company policy. He should merely have asked her to accompany him to my office.' He smiled wryly. 'He was over-enthusiastic in his work, I'm afraid.'

'You find that funny, do you?' Caro erupted.

Gil looked at her, and frowned. 'Of course not!'

'He was a thug, and you know it!'

Gil's rage began to show through his charm, she was glad to see, like tin showing through the gilding on a cheap bracelet. He had to struggle to keep the smile on his face and his eyes distinctly menaced her.

He saw he wasn't deceiving her, so he turned his charm back to her father, spoke to him confidentially, appealing to him as a fellow store owner. 'You know how it is these days. There has been a big increase in theft from the store, we have had to have cameras fitted on all floors, and a staff sitting in front of the monitors all the time. If you had seen the video film of the way your daughter acted in the store this morning, you would understand why my security staff's suspicions were aroused. She was clearly up to something, she was acting so oddly; they assumed she was another shoplifter.' He threw Caro a narrow-eyed glance. 'It didn't occur to them that she was just an industrial spy.'

'Oh, don't be ridiculous!' Caro muttered.

'It's the only word I can think of!' he snapped.

Caro gritted her teeth, very flushed. She wasn't getting into another squabble with him, especially in front of his grandmother.

Her father slid her a sideways, enquiring look, and she shook her head at him.

Lady Westbrook was looking thunderstruck. 'What?' she demanded. 'What are you talking about, Gil? What happened at the store this morning? You didn't tell me anything about a problem.'

'It was a little misunderstanding!' he dismissed.

Fred gave Caro an uncertain look, signalling his doubts about how to proceed. If there was a possibility of buying Westbrooks they certainly didn't want to wreck their chances by suing the store, but Fred knew how angry Caro was about what had happened to her, and he was angry himself. His eyes asked her what she wanted him to do, and she grimaced back at him, recognising their dilemma and silently telling him to forget it. Getting hold of Westbrooks was more important than getting her revenge on Gil Martell.

'It was all cleared up, Lady Westbrook,' she said. 'It was just a mistake, as your grandson says—and he did apologise.'

Gil Martell gave her a grim little smile, mockery in those dark eyes. 'I'm glad you've decided to accept my apology, Miss Ramsgate. Very rational of you. I had a hunch you were going to make my life difficult. I'm glad I was wrong.'

'Caro is always sensible,' her father boasted, and Gil Martell's brows curved in derision.

'Sensible?' He swept her from head to foot with another of those lethal glances of his, smiling with dry amusement. 'Yes, I suppose that is an apt description of her. I'm sure she's very...' He paused, then said softly, 'Sensible!'

Caro's grey eyes hated him; she knew he was making fun of her and she wished she weren't inhibited by the presence of his grandmother, and the vital importance of the deal her father hoped to make with Lady Westbrook, but she couldn't risk answering back, so she bit down on her inner lip and held her tongue.

'No answer?' Gil laughed. 'Very wise.' He looked at his watch and shrugged. 'In that case, I must go now, I have an important engagement.'

'Who with?' his grandmother demanded.

His expression was bland. 'I don't imagine you know her, Grandmother.'

Lady Westbrook's frown carved deep lines into her forehead. 'Not Miranda, then...?'

Gil gave her an icy, angry glance, without answering the question, and turned away to give Caro a little bow. 'Goodnight, Miss Ramsgate.' He nodded to her father. 'Mr Ramsgate. I hope you enjoy your evening.'

Caro thought for a second that he was going to leave without saying goodbye to his grandmother, but he bent and kissed Lady Westbrook's cheek. 'Goodnight, dear,' he said levelly, and walked away before she could answer him.

The door closed behind him and Lady Westbrook sighed. 'He is my only grandchild,' she said quietly, without looking at either Caro or her father. Neither of them liked to reply. What could they say? They had the distinct feeling she had forgotten they were there.

Who was he meeting tonight? wondered Caro as she ate a very good dinner, and drank the excellent wine served with it. If the gossip columns were to be believed, he dated any number of women—mostly very attractive ones. It was none of her business, and it was stupid to be curious about him. He would never be interested in her, so what difference did it make to her who he was meeting? But she wished she knew whether he was seeing the Countess again—how serious was that affair? Had her husband had good reason for picking a fight with Gil Martell? Caro pulled herself up, and told herself not to be such a fool, and to think about something else.

It was on their way home that her father said to her, 'She's disinheriting him.'

Caro stared, her grey eyes wide. 'Do you think so? She didn't say that. Just because she sells the store, it doesn't mean she's cutting him out of her will.'

'It means she's taking away from him what he has spent years working for,' Fred Ramsgate drily said. 'You saw how he took it.'

'Badly.'

'Precisely. He knows she is disinheriting him, taking the store away from him. Maybe she still intends to leave him her money, but by then it will be too late. He will have lost the store he already thinks of as his own. His family built the place, after all. They've owned it for generations. No wonder Gil Martell is furious.'

Caro gave her father a curious, sideways look. 'You seem to sympathise with him!'

'I have a sneaking fellow-feeling,' Fred wryly agreed. 'He's done a good job with the store. His father left it in a bad way and he's turned it round, only to have his grandmother fly into a temper with him and decide to sell the place over his head. Yes, I sympathise with the man.'

'But you're still going to buy his store?' Caro asked rhetorically; she was certain her father would go ahead and buy Westbrooks. He had never let personal feelings cloud his judgement or influence him in the past—why should he do so now?

'Of course,' said Fred flatly. 'If I don't buy it, someone else will—and I want Westbrooks badly. I learnt long ago, Caro, that when you make a deal like this, the chances are that somebody will get hurt in the process. In business, you can't afford to worry over every little detail of the consequences of a deal.'

Caro grimaced. 'I suppose you're right. Dad, do you think she's doing it because of the gossip in the paper this morning? The fight in the nightclub?'

'Who knows?' Fred shrugged. 'He seemed to think that that was why, didn't he?'

'Yes, but... well, isn't that petty of her? She doesn't seem the petty type, but...'

'There may be other reasons we don't know about, Caro. Who knows why she suddenly wants to sell? Maybe she needs the cash? Maybe she wants to settle money on someone other than her grandson? Perhaps she's in debt? It isn't our affair. That's exactly what I meant about not worrying about the consequences of a deal. Why Lady Westbrook is selling is nothing to do with us. Our only concern is getting the best possible deal for our shareholders. We'll look at their books, study the accounts, make sure the store is worth the price they're asking. The rest isn't our problem.'

'We're going to need Gil Martell's co-operation,' Caro murmured wryly, 'and I don't see us getting it, do you?'

'It will be your team that goes in there to look at the books,' her father pointed out. 'You'll just have to find a way of persuading Martell to play ball.'

'Oh, thanks!' she groaned. 'Thanks a lot!'

Ten days later she sat in her office staring at the phone, nerving herself to ring Gil Martell at Westbrooks. Before real discussions on the take-over could start, her father wanted his own accountants to go over the books and report on the situation in the store, but Lady Westbrook's lawyers had made it clear that Gil Martell was, as Caro had anticipated, being difficult. He wouldn't hand over the accounts and he had ignored all requests to allow Caro and her team into the accounts department at the store.

The market value of the shares was temptingly priced, but wasn't enough to make Fred Ramsgate feel happy about buying a controlling interest without ever getting sight of the actual accounts. He wanted to be sure he was acquiring a valuable property at the right price; he did not want to discover that he had paid more than the store was really worth.

'You talk to him!' he had said that morning. 'We've tried approaching him formally, through his own people. Now try the direct approach. Ring him yourself.'

Caro reached a hand towards the phone and dialled. She got through to Gil's office at once and spoke to a secretary with a remote, indifferent voice.

No, she was informed, Mr Martell was not available. He was in a meeting. No, his secretary did not know when he would be free. She reluctantly agreed to take a message asking him to ring Caro back.

He didn't, of course. Caro rang again, got the same cold, distant voice. He still wasn't available. She left a message. 'You will make sure he gets it? It is important. And urgent.'

The secretary sounded about as impressed as she might have been by a fly buzzing around her office, and no doubt would have liked to deal with Caro the way she would deal with a fly.

Caro felt like yelling down the phone at her, just to make her jump, but could not risk it. She had to pretend to be sweetness and light until she finally managed to get hold of Gil Martell.

He still didn't ring back. She tried again and again over the next two days, getting angrier each time, with the same result. His secretary's cold voice took on a smug note. She was enjoying the process. Probably, Gil Martell was enjoying himself, too. That made two of them. Caro was not having fun.

'Any joy?' her father asked, putting his head round her door on the third morning.

'None,' she grimly told him, grabbing up her handbag and walking purposefully towards him.

'Where are you going?' asked Fred, backing to let her through the door.

'Where I should have gone in the first place. Westbrooks.'

'Good luck!' Fred called after her as she made for the lift. He was relieved that it wasn't he who had to deal with Gil Martell. Dealing with Lady Westbrook would be ordeal enough for Fred when the time came. He was saving his energy.

Caro didn't attempt to go straight up to the managing director's office when she reached Westbrooks. She began on the ground floor and made a deliberately slow progress from counter to counter, from floor to floor, making notes, watching a demonstration in the make-up department, checking out a new perfume on special offer, tasting a French cheese in the food hall, studying a display of new German kitchen equipment on the home and garden floor, fingering towels and sheets, checking chinaware and glass, radio sets and the latest electronic robot in the toy department.

She was cruising slowly around the fashion floor when she spotted a black dress of elegant cut and style by her favourite designer. Caro loved it on sight, and just had to try it on.

She took it into a fitting-room and was standing in the cubicle in her slip, bra and panties when somebody pulled back the curtain. Caro jumped, staring into the mirror in startled surprise, and saw Gil Martell's angry face reflected behind her own.

'OK, what are you up to?' he bit out.

Behind him, Caro saw faces—the assistant who was in charge of the fitting-rooms, a middle-aged customer with a dress over her arm. Turning pink, Caro crossly said, 'Pull that curtain back! There are people staring!'

Gil glanced into the mirror, frowningly saw their audience, but instead of drawing the curtain and leaving her alone he stepped into the cubicle and joined her, pulling the curtain to isolate them both. Outside they heard the others hurriedly walking away.

Caro backed, suddenly breathless. The tiny space seemed much tinier with Gil in it. He dominated it and made her even more conscious of being half naked.

'Go away,' she said shakily, turning her back on him, but that didn't help because Gil watched her in the mirror, standing right behind her. He was wearing a formal dark suit, pin-striped, expensively tailored, with a tight-fitting waistcoat beneath the open jacket; but the formality couldn't hide that assertive masculinity.

'Oh, no, not until you tell me what you're doing, hanging around here again!' he said, staring at the reflection of her body, the smooth, creamy skin, the pale shoulders, full, round breasts in their lacy cups, the silky expanse of waist and hip beneath the transparent white slip. His eyes moved downward to the outline of her tiny briefs, the long, slim thighs, and Caro began to tremble, and was angry with herself. Why did he make her feel this way? If this was a beach she wouldn't be embarrassed by lying about in far less than she was wearing now. Why did it make her go hot and cold to have Gil Martell staring at her?

She grabbed up her dress and held it in front of herself. 'You wouldn't answer my phone calls. This was the only way I could think of to make you take some notice of me!'

His dark eyes glittered. 'You want me to take notice of you? Well, I wouldn't want to disappoint you when you're so desperate for my attention.'

Caro turned scarlet. 'I didn't mean that, and you know I didn't——' She broke off with a cry of shock as his arms came round her.

'Don't!'

With one hand he snatched her dress away and dropped it on a chair, while the other hand stroked softly, lingeringly, down her body, from breast to thigh. She couldn't stop or conceal the shaking of her limbs, the heated blood filling her face.

Outside the cubicle a new customer had arrived; they heard the clip of her footsteps, the swish of the curtain rings.

'Let go of me! Go away and let me get dressed!' Caro whispered, afraid of making a scene in public. She couldn't get over the shock and embarrassment of being dragged through the store by his detective the other day. She had thought that, when Gil knew she was in Westbrooks again, he would have come rushing down to find her and order her to come to his office. She certainly hadn't expected him to act like this. 'How dare you touch me? Let go,' she muttered.

Gil didn't answer, he didn't let go of her; he smiled at her in the mirror, a taunting, derisive smile, as he moved in closer, his body pressing against her back, his head lowered to her bare shoulder, his mouth cool and tantalising on her skin.

'You have a lovely body,' he said softly. 'Very sexy.' His fingers slid inside the silk and lace to caress her warm breasts and Caro caught her breath, shuddering with helpless pleasure.

Gil was watching her in the mirror; he could read the betraying signals, the parted lips, the quickened breathing, the colour coming and going, the faint but visible trembling, and mockery gleamed in his dark eyes.

'But tempting though you are, I'm busy today, so I'll have to get back to work, I'm afraid,' he drawled, letting go of her.

Humiliation and relief fought in Caro's mind; she stumbled away from him, tremblingly picked up her dress again and began struggling into it, avoiding his watching amusement.

'The first time I saw you, I disliked you, Mr Martell,' she said thickly. 'The second time I met you, I disliked you even more, and now I realise you are not going to improve on closer acquaintance. On the contrary—I'm fast deciding that I hate the sight of you.'

He laughed. 'Odd, that wasn't the impression you gave just now.'

Her colour darkened, and she bit her lip.

'And I don't hate the sight of you,' he went on in that mocking voice. 'Especially the way you looked before you put that dress back on! Do you have to? I prefer you without it. I wouldn't call you pretty, but you have a terrific figure; all those lovely, rich curves in the right places.'

'Oh, shut up!' she hissed. 'And keep your voice down!' She fumbled in her bag, found a comb and tidied her hair, fighting to stop her hands shaking. No man had ever had such a violent effect on her; she couldn't understand it.

Gil Martell drew back the curtain and Caro picked up the black dress and walked out of the cubicle without looking at him. The assistant on duty stared avidly as Caro handed her the black dress, muttering that she didn't want it. How much of what went on in the cubicle had the other girl overheard? It was so embarrassing— Caro couldn't wait to get away; she felt as if everyone around there were watching her and Gil and whispering.

They took the lift up to his office, neither of them speaking. His secretary gave Caro a frigid, hostile look as they walked past her desk.

'You've had several urgent calls, sir,' she said to Gil. 'I've left a note of them on your pad.'

He nodded briskly. 'Thank you. Hold all calls for the moment, will you, however urgent.'

He closed the door and walked across his own office to his desk, sank into the chair and gestured to Caro to take the seat on the other side. She sat down, crossing her long legs, and he watched the movement far too closely.

'Well? What can I do for you?' he asked, and he used the words deliberately—it was another tease, one she resented, and she glared at him.

'I'm tired of playing games——'

'I'm not,' he purred.

'I am not flirting with you, Mr Martell!' she flared up, very flushed.

He pointedly glanced at his watch. 'Well, whatever you're doing, Miss Ramsgate, hurry up—because I'm a very busy man.'

'Then stop having fun at my expense,' Caro snapped. 'Stop pretending you don't know why I'm here. You're well aware why I've been ringing you. Until we see the books, we can't proceed with this negotiation. I want you to let me and my team spend a few days here going over the accounts with your people.'

'Why should I?' he asked tersely, the amusement disappearing from his dark eyes.

'Because if you don't do it voluntarily, your grandmother will make you hand over the books by legal means,' Caro threatened, losing her temper, and then wished she hadn't said that because she had no authority to threaten him with any such thing. If he told his grandmother what she had said to him, Lady Westbrook might pull out of the negotiations. She lowered her eyes, while watching him uneasily through her lashes, and saw his features tighten, his mouth a stiff pale line, his eyes hard.

There was a long silence, then he said in an expressionless voice, 'Very well, the books will be made available to you from tomorrow morning at nine o'clock, but they must not leave this building. I will see to it that office space is free for you and your team to use, and you will go over the books here, without removing them or copying them or in any way making notes from them. Is that understood?'

'Yes.' She understood. He was giving in because he thought he had no option; but he was not going to make it easy for her, or the accountants she brought with her. 'You can trust me to keep my word,' she added coolly.

Gil's eyes flicked contemptuously to her. 'Trust you? Do you think I'm that stupid? Oh, no, Miss Ramsgate, I don't trust either you or your piranha of a father—which is why I am going to have you right here, in this office, under my eyes, while you're working on my accounts. I'll have a desk moved in; telephones, computers, whatever you need to do your job. But I'll be here, too, watching you, every minute of the day and night.'

Caro stared at him, feeling oddly under threat. She did not know if she could stand the ordeal of spending that much time alone in here with Gil Martell.

CHAPTER FOUR

THE first morning, Caro didn't see much of Gil, as it turned out, because he was out of the office on his usual tour of the store to talk to the various supervisors and floor managers and check on any problems or worries they had. His secretary silently cleared his desk of every scrap of paper, when he had gone, locking most of the material into his desk or a filing cabinet, while Caro drily watched her through her lashes. The other woman didn't say anything, but she didn't need to—she was making it all too plain that she did not trust Caro an inch.

Caro and her team spent that morning talking to the store's accounts manager, who treated them remotely, with reluctance, as if they were germs he might catch. His manner to Caro was lofty, slightly incredulous—his eyes made it clear that he couldn't believe she was any good at her job; she was too young, for one thing, and, for another, she was a woman. He, of course, was middle-aged, a short, stout man with a little black moustache above his prim lips. Caro had met men like him all her working life, men who could not believe she had brains and who suspected she owed her job to her father. Men like Gil Martell, for instance.

Once Caro had got everything she wanted from him, she coolly dismissed him, and she and her team settled down to extract every last ounce of information from the accounts. She could learn all about a company in an amazingly short time, deduce from what she saw what was being kept hidden and focus on all the problem areas and loss-making departments. She knew it wouldn't take her long to draw up a detailed profile of the company.

No doubt everyone knew, by now, that the store might be about to change hands, and the staff must be very worried. People always were when they heard of a change of ownership. They felt their jobs might be threatened, and Caro could understand their anxieties; she sympathised with them, although she couldn't say so without disloyalty to her father. So she just did her own job, although she often wondered when her father would at last be satisfied and stop his empire-building.

When Gil Martell did arrive that morning it was a brief visit before lunch, and he was polite and distant, which suited Caro. She preferred not to have him around while she did her job.

That first day was typical of the days which followed. She realised very quickly that Gil was not the type of managing director who sat in his office all day, or who delegated. He was out of his office as much as he was in it, and he certainly both worked hard and did not delegate. She soon began to know his routine, and, of course, she set up a routine of her own.

At noon each day, her staff went to lunch, but Caro stayed at work. She brought food with her: a light snack, a tub of cottage cheese, perhaps, some rye crispbreads and an apple, and a bottle of sparkling mineral water. Gil Martell usually went out to lunch; she gathered from what she overheard that he lunched important clients, suppliers, importers.

Around the fourth day, Gil Martell came back while she was in the middle of her snack. 'Is that all you're having for lunch?' he enquired, inspecting the remains of her meal. 'You can use the staff canteen if you want to; they do a very good meal.'

'I prefer to bring my own, thanks.'

'Suit yourself.' He shrugged.

'I always do,' Caro assured him, and he showed her his teeth in an angry smile.

'I believe you.'

The air bristled, their eyes quarrelled, then Gil turned away and strode over to his own desk. He sat down, opened a locked drawer, and began skimming through the pile of documents he extracted. Caro forced herself to look down at her own work, tried to concentrate on it, but she was nervously conscious of him, on the other side of the room. She kept remembering what had happened between them in that fitting-room—his hands on her body, his lips moving softly on her bare skin. Each time the image flashed through her mind she felt heat flare up inside her. She fought to control her breathing, afraid that he might hear her, guess what she was thinking about.

The phone rang and she jumped, then automatically stretched out her hand to answer it. 'Yes?'

Out of the corner of her eye she caught sight of Gil's hand on the phone on his own desk and realised he had been going to take the call, too.

'Reception desk,' said the voice in her ear. 'The Countess of Jurby is here and would like to see Mr Martell. Shall I send her up?'

'Hold on,' Caro said, lowered the receiver and looked briefly at Gil. 'It's for you.'

He picked up his own phone; Caro hung up and pretended to be engrossed in her work, but out of the corner of her eye she watched him.

'Yes? What?' He frowned, his fingers tapping his desk, then said, 'Yes, put her on.' There was a pause, then he said in a low voice, 'What on earth are you doing here? You know Colin will go crazy if he finds out!'

Caro couldn't help listening, knowing that he was talking to that woman, the one who had caused the fight in the nightclub, and because of that had made Gil's grandmother decide to sell Westbrooks. Was Gil the Countess's lover? Was she planning to divorce her husband to marry Gil? Caro's computer made a shrill sound and she bit her lip crossly, realising she had made a stupid mistake, mis-keyed a whole line of figures.

She wasn't concentrating. Concentrate! she ordered herself. Stop eavesdropping on conversations which aren't your business!

'You're leaving him?' Gil's voice rose, then he took a deep breath. 'Wait down there, I'll join you in two minutes.'

He slammed the phone down and stood up. Caro kept her eyes riveted on her computer. So the Countess was leaving her husband? Was Gil running to her eagerly, or in panic? Did he want her to be free, or was he appalled by the idea? He had had so many other women; was this one different?

He came past her desk and halted. She felt his eyes like lasers and warily looked up.

'You won't repeat any private conversations you hear in this office,' he warned, his lips barely parting to let the words out, his face harsh with menace.

She smiled coolly, and didn't bother to answer, hoping to infuriate him. She did.

'Do you hear me?' he snarled, voice rising.

'I should think everyone in the store can!' Caro snapped back.

'Working in my office, you're in a privileged position——' he began and she interrupted, impatiently.

'It was you who insisted that I work in here! It wasn't my idea!'

'You probably put it into my head,' he muttered, scowling.

'Oh, don't be so ridiculous!'

He had a brooding look on his face. 'Women are good at doing that. They plant ideas in a man's subconscious and then let him imagine he thought of them all by himself! Look at Adam and Eve. Adam would never have thought of eating that apple if Eve hadn't whispered in his ear.'

'I didn't whisper in your ear; I didn't want to share this office with you! In fact, I'd be very happy to move out right now, if it's bothering you to have me here!'

'I didn't say it bothered me!' He turned those deep dark eyes on her and Caro began to feel oddly dizzy. 'If you ever start to bother me you'll soon know it, don't worry,' Gil drawled.

Caro had to look away, break the spell of that hypnotic stare before the room spun round in front of her eyes.

There was a long pause, then he said, 'At the moment, all I want is to be sure you won't mention, to your father, or anyone else, anything you overhear while you're in this office.'

'I resent the suggestion that I might,' she burst out, her head coming up again and her grey eyes flashing. 'I learnt discretion at a very early age. My father's business dealings are always secret; if so much as a whisper got out, it could be disastrous and could cost us a great deal of money. I soon understood that I mustn't repeat anything I heard, and I assure you I never gossip, Mr Martell.'

'Then you're a very unusual woman,' he said with dry cynicism, turned away and walked to the door.

Caro watched the long, supple line of his back, the arrogant carriage of that black head. He moved with an almost animal grace, she thought, her mouth dry for some reason. He glanced back and at once she looked down at the desk again, breathing audibly—at least, to herself. He probably couldn't hear her. Or could he?

'See you later,' Gil said in an odd, soft voice, charged with something—amusement or threat, she couldn't be sure which.

She didn't answer and a second later the door closed. Caro leaned back in her chair, angry with herself for letting him get to her again. How on earth had it happened, this time? She had been angry with him one minute and breathless the next, and it was without rhyme or reason. She was going crazy; it was the only explanation.

He was always far too quick at noticing her reactions, too. That was even more worrying. You might almost think he could read her mind, and that made her shiver. Was he on her wavelength? Could he sense what was happening inside her? Or was it just that women were always reacting to him like that? The gossip columns certainly gave that impression; they seemed fascinated by Gil Martell's relationships with women, which were so much more interesting than his business dealings. She had been reading snippets about him ever since that fight in the nightclub. Past scandals had been resurrected, his old flames recalled—and there had been quite a few. If you could believe the gutter Press, Gil Martell was some sort of modern Don Juan.

Well, if he thought she was yet another female flipping over him, he was very wrong! Caro didn't know why she was having these odd symptoms whenever Gil was around, but it wasn't because she was falling for him, and if he imagined it was, she would soon put him right— and tell him a few home truths at the same time. The conceit of the man was maddening. Did he think he was irresistible? He probably did, for which her own sex was partly to blame. From all she had read about him in the papers, women had been chasing him since he left school, and not because he was wealthy. Gil Martell had sex appeal, and knew it, damn him.

She tried to get back to work, but she was so irritated, so uneasy, that she couldn't concentrate; she couldn't even sit still, she had to get up and walk about, mentally going over the various things she was dying to say to Gil Martell. After a few moments of disturbed prowling, she came to a standstill at the window, registering for the first time that the spring had finally begun, without her noticing until now. The sky was blue, the sun was shining, somewhere a bird was singing and the trees had broken into leaf. She struggled with the catch and opened the window to let in air which was warm on her skin, fragrant with the scent of flowers.

Perhaps that was why she was so edgy? she rather desperately thought, clutching at straws. It was spring making her restless, putting ideas into her head—but why ideas about a man she didn't even like? Perhaps it was simply that Gil Martell had happened to be the first man she'd seen while she was in this mood? Any man would have had the same effect. It just happened to have been Gil. And when her strange restlessness passed she would get over Gil Martell and wonder what she had ever seen in him.

Spring was deceptive and dangerous, she decided, taking her entranced gaze hurriedly away from the blue, seductive sky and glancing down into the grey, all too down to earth London street.

And that was how she saw them together, Gil and the Countess, on the pavement, talking, while a black London taxi waited, the driver leaning on his window and looking impatient. Caro couldn't see the woman's face, just her blonde hair and that slender figure in the white mink jacket and sleek black suit. Hadn't she been a model before she married the Earl of Jurby? She had that sort of body: skinny, flat, tall. Was that the sort of figure Gil Martell liked his women to have?

The Countess put a hand on Gil's arm and the scarlet of her nails gleamed like blood in the spring sunlight, then she stood on her toes to lean forward and kiss him on the mouth. Gil's hand came up to grip her shoulder.

Caro swung away from the window, her mouth tight. It looked as if the gossip had been accurate and they were lovers. There had been such intimacy in the way they had gazed into each other's eyes; that wasn't how friends looked at each other. The kiss had come as no surprise after that, but she couldn't stop seeing the other woman's red mouth, the way her hand had rested on his arm, the way he had caught hold of her.

Oh, yes, they had to be lovers. Not that it mattered a row of beans to her, of course. Why should it? Her own feelings about him were all moonshine, a spring fever which should soon be over. She marched back to her desk and sat down, trying to focus her mind on the accounts but waiting all the time to hear Gil return.

When he did come he let the door slam behind him and she jumped, her grey eyes flying wide open. He stared at her in surprise and she felt she had to explain her obvious shock.

'Oh... it's you...' she mumbled.

'Who did you think it was going to be?' Gil drily answered, going to his own desk and throwing himself into his chair with an impatient gesture. 'This is turning out to be one hell of a day, and all the complications start and end with women.'

'I'm sure you know how to deal with them!' muttered Caro, bending over her work and trying to look utterly engrossed in that.

'What?' he demanded irritably. 'What did you say?'

'Nothing,' she said, and wished it were true—she shouldn't talk to him at all, it would be much safer.

Gil Martell obviously agreed because he snarled, 'Good, then keep it that way! I'm in no mood to listen to comments from you.'

Caro shut her mouth firmly on what she wanted to shout back. She kept her eyes on the computer screen on which she was working and fed more facts and figures into it. A picture was already beginning to emerge, but it would be days before she could tell her father precisely what he needed to know.

Gil Martell made a series of brisk, matter-of-fact phone calls around the building, then left the office without a word. Caro was relieved to see him go. When he was there she couldn't stop being aware of him. It was infuriating. She had worked with men throughout her career without such a problem cropping up before, but suddenly when this one man was in the same room she felt her very skin prickling with uneasy awareness, and she did not like it.

She worked very late that evening. Gil Martell returned to his office just before seven o'clock, long after the store had closed and the vast majority of the sales assistants and clerical workers, including all her own team of accountants, had gone home; and stopped in his tracks, seeing her still there.

'You can't stay here any longer.' He frowned. 'The night security staff will be coming on duty in five minutes and they will expect the building to be empty. If you're here it will interfere with the automatic alarm system, which is due to come on at seven-thirty. It's too complicated to make exceptions, even for me, so you must leave.'

She leaned back in her chair, unconsciously massaging her neck with one hand, as she always did when she was getting tired. 'I wanted to finish this section of the accounts before I broke off,' she protested, knowing she was not sorry to have to stop.

'It will just have to wait,' Gil impatiently said. He looked at his watch. 'You've been working since eight o'clock this morning—eleven hours! Do you get overtime?'

She laughed, relaxing briefly, her grey eyes amused by the idea. 'I'm one of the family, remember. I've never even thought of asking Dad for overtime.'

'I hope he pays you a good salary, then.'

'He pays me what he would pay anyone doing my job,' she said, immediately touchy, suspecting Gil was criticising her father, and ready to resent it.

'But no overtime,' he said drily.

'My father expects me to work the way he does—with a hundred per cent of his attention. If I were a clock-watcher, he'd be disappointed in me.'

His dark eyes were intent and thoughtful, unnervingly shrewd. 'And you'd hate to disappoint your father?'

She didn't answer. Gil Martell was taking too close an interest in her thought processes and Caro did not like it. He didn't press the matter. He came round the desk to stare at the screen of her computer; studying the immaculate rows of figures. His brows drew together, and she watched him, wondering if he hated to have her investigating his accounts as much as she disliked having him try to probe her mind. She had met this reaction in some businessmen before. They seemed to feel that having her look through their accounts was almost like having her strip them naked.

'This is all it means to you and your father, isn't it?' he suddenly bit out, his eyes smouldering. 'Just accounts like these—figures in a ledger, profit and loss, the chance to make even more money than you have already. You make me so furious! It's time you realised that an old family business like mine means a damn sight more than that.'

'I know,' Caro said wearily. 'Your family built the business up from nothing, and you don't want it going out of your hands——'

'I wasn't going to say that,' Gil snapped. 'I'm talking about people, people who've often worked here for a whole lifetime; maybe they are the second or third generation in a family to work here—grandfather, father and son, mother and daughter, making a commitment to the store, like myself, like my father and grandfather before me.'

'Hardly the same, is it?' Caro drily asked him. 'After all, your family own the place, naturally you feel strongly about it, but your employees may not feel quite the same way. I'm sure they want to keep their jobs, but I doubt if they care much who runs the store, so long as they are still getting paid.'

'You think that's all they care about?' he retorted, his brows black above those angry eyes. 'Their pay-packet at the end of the month? You underestimate them. It isn't a question of loyalty to me, or my family. They have strong views about the way the store is managed because they really care about the store itself, they feel part of it, especially, of course, those who have been here for a number of years and hope to stay with us.'

'And, of course, you always ask their opinion before you take any decision?' Caro said with a sarcastic little smile.

'They're fully involved in policy-making,' he snapped. 'We have a management committee on which all departments are represented and they're very forthright with their comments and suggestions. Very helpful, too; they often come up with an idea we haven't even considered, and if it works they get a bonus. Our bonus scheme has been very popular. I instituted it when I took over. It was part of my attempt to turn the business around from loss to profit, involving the staff as much as possible.' He broke off, frowning, then said flatly, 'Some of the staff actually own shares they took instead of a cash bonus. We gave them that choice. The younger ones preferred cash, I found; it was those who had been with us for years who took shares. But if you want to know what they think, instead of feeding mathematics into your computer you should be coming round the store with me to meet some of them. Then maybe you would realise what a store like Westbrooks means in human terms.'

'I don't need to be told that!' Caro said, rather stunned by his outburst, but still resentful of the accusation of being strictly mercenary. 'I grew up in this business, just as much as you did. I know how vital the workforce is;

Dad still gets Christmas cards from people who worked for him in our original family store up North, people he's known most of his life and thinks of as friends, not employees. Whenever he's up there he calls in to have a chat with them. Dad taught me that you can't run a business successfully unless your staff trust and like you.'

'You quote your father as if he were God,' Gil Martell mocked and she flushed, but at that moment, out of the corner of her eye, she saw a shadow on the frosted glass of the office door, and stiffened, staring.

'There's somebody out there, listening to us!' she whispered and Gil looked quickly in that direction, frowning. A second later there was a knock on the door.

'Come in!' Gil called.

A uniformed security guard appeared in the doorway, nodding to them. 'Evening, Mr Martell. Miss.' His eyes were curious. 'Sorry to interrupt you, but the automatic system comes on in ten minutes, I'm afraid. If you're working late, I shall have to escort you out of the building when you go, remember.'

'We're going now, don't worry.' Gil glanced at Caro. 'Sign off your computer, will you, Miss Ramsgate?' he politely requested, leaving her no option but to do as he asked.

She obeyed in silence, carefully closed down her computer, and locked away all the material on the desk—documents, computer discs, ledgers—while the two men watched her. The guard then escorted them to the lift, along the silent corridor. Caro only then realised how empty the great building was, and how eerie it seemed at night with most of the lights dimmed and every little sound echoing along the maze of corridors.

She shivered as she stepped into the lift, and Gil gave her a narrow-eyed look. 'Cold? I'm not surprised, in that!' He let his gaze drift down over the charcoal-grey jersey dress and jacket she wore, making the back of her neck prickle with awareness. 'You look very good in it,' Gil drawled, his stare lingering on the way the jersey clung to her breasts, and she angrily felt heat stir inside her body. 'But it can't be very warm.'

It wasn't. She had wanted to look smart and efficient, and hadn't cared that the outfit was thin and light-weight. She certainly hadn't wanted to invite him to notice her figure, but of course she couldn't tell him that because to do so would be to admit that she was in-tensely conscious of having him stare at her. 'It was quite warm this morning!' she defended herself.

He shrugged. 'I know it's April but the weather is still treacherous. Well, once you're in your car you can put on the heating.'

That reminded her that she had intended to ring for a taxi before leaving the office tonight, and she made an irritated face.

'What now?' asked Gil, still watching her.

'I don't drive in, unless I come with my father,' she explained. 'I usually take the Underground, or go by bus. It simply isn't worth the hassle of taking a car, and our house is only ten minutes away from the office. To-night I meant to call a cab, as I was working so late, but I forgot. Never mind, there are usually taxis cruising past.'

'I'll give you a lift home,' he offered at once, as she should have anticipated, but his tone was dry. Did he suspect she had been dropping hints? That idea made her furious.

'That's very kind,' she said coldly. 'But I'm certain to get a taxi at once.'

'Don't be stupid. Your house is on my route home,' he insisted. As they left the lift, he took her by the elbow and guided her firmly through the store to a private exit guarded by another of the security staff. Gil Martell nodded to him, smiled and said, 'Goodnight,' and then they walked through the open door, hearing the door being locked behind them before they had taken two steps across the pavement.

The gleaming black Rolls-Royce was parked right outside, waiting for him. Caro gave it a look, then stared anxiously up and down the street in search of a taxi. Typically, there wasn't one in sight, and she found herself a moment later being put into the front passenger seat.

They drove away northwards through London's brilliantly lit streets towards the quieter district of Regents Park, with its Georgian terraces and elegant gardens.

'Do up your seatbelt!' Gil ordered, drawing up at the traffic-lights in Baker Street a moment later. Caro had forgotten to do so in her state of nerves; she pulled the belt across her middle and tried to slot it into position, but her fingers were all thumbs and after watching her briefly Gil leant over to do it for her, his fingers brushing against hers. She stiffened as that lean, muscled body came so close that she picked up the male scent of his skin and felt his thigh touch her own. A wave of sexual awareness rose inside her and she shifted away from the contact with him. What was the matter with her?

He deftly clicked home the seatbelt, straightened, eyeing her with narrow observation and then appalled her by asking, 'Are you always this scared of men?'

Hot colour rolled up her face. 'I'm not scared of you!'

'Then why do you jump about ten feet in the air every time I come too close?'

'I don't!'

He laughed and leaned towards her, and she couldn't stop herself tensing, moving further away, an agitated pulse beating in her throat, at her temples.

'No?' he drawled, his mouth curling with derision.

Caro stared straight ahead, fighting with panic. 'The lights have turned green!'

Gil laughed. 'What a relief! Saved by traffic-lights!' But he turned his attention to the road all the same, and the car smoothly rolled away.

Caro stared at the orange street lights on either side of them, her eyes dazzled by the brilliance. She was furious, both with herself and Gil Martell. She wasn't naïve enough to imagine he was interested in her as a woman. She knew she wasn't sexually attractive; she had learnt that very early in her life, been bitterly convinced that the only reason a man might pursue her was for her father's money, especially a man like Gil Martell, who could pick and choose his women.

He fancied women like the Countess of Jurby—blonde, fashionable, skinny as boys. He had been teasing her, just now, using his sexual power as a weapon in this war against her and her father, and she had been stupid enough to let him see he could reach her. She had to do something about her spring fever in a hurry. She didn't know why Gil Martell affected her the way he did, but it had to stop at once.

They were in the leafy streets of Regents Park, just a few minutes away from her home. From the zoo in the park itself could be heard strange, distant, animal sounds which, at night, sounded oddly menacing and yet mournful. She shivered as she heard them; they seemed to echo her own feelings.

Gil drove past his grandmother's house, then suddenly braked with a screech of tyres on the road, sending

Caro tumbling forward. Her seatbelt saved her from injury, but she turned an angry face towards him.

'What on earth are you doing?'

He didn't answer; he was too busy staring at a car parked on the driveway—a red Porsche, noted Caro. She watched Gil curiously.

'What's wrong?'

His face had a dark, brooding impatience. 'It's Miranda's car,' he muttered. 'I told her to go to her mother's—why in the name of all that's holy didn't she do that? If Colin comes looking for her and finds her here, he'll kill both of us.'

'Maybe that wouldn't be such a bad idea!' Caro said, feeling vicious all of a sudden, but he did not seem to be listening to her, he was much too intent on his own thoughts. If he hadn't been, he wouldn't be blurting all this out to her, of course. He wouldn't have breathed a syllable if he weren't so taken aback.

'But why come to my grandmother?' he thought aloud. 'And what is Grandmother up to, letting her stay?'

'She could just be having dinner here!' pointed out Caro in a flat, cool voice, and he looked sharply at her, this time as if he actually saw her.

'Which means my grandmother invited her! But why should she do that? She can't stand Miranda.'

'When you've dropped me off at my home you can come back here and find out!' she said, glancing at her watch in a meaningful way. 'As you say, it is dinnertime, and I am hungry.'

His dark eyes narrowed on her, his mouth indented. 'Yes,' he said slowly, and Caro was not too happy about the way he said that, or the way he was watching her. There was distinct calculation in his deep voice, in those gleaming eyes. 'You're hungry,' he repeated, and she nodded.

'Very, and my father likes his dinner promptly at eight, which was five minutes ago, and I'll be too late to eat with him if I don't get home soon, so could you please——' Her voice broke off as Gil started his engine again, but instead of driving on he swung the wheel and reversed over the pavement, into his grandmother's driveway, parking alongside the red Porsche.

'What are you doing?' Caro bust out in alarm.

'Taking you to dinner with my grandmother,' he blandly informed her, sliding out of the driver's seat and coming round to open the door for her.

She shook her head in violent refusal. 'No, I can't...she didn't invite me... Don't be ridiculous...'

Gil leaned over her and she shrank back from him, confused and flushed, but all he did was unbuckle her seatbelt.

'Out you get!' he briskly ordered.

'I'm not coming in, take me home! Go away!' Caro didn't know how to deal with the situation. Gil had an obstinate look to him. He tried to take her arm and pull her out but she pushed him back. 'Will you leave me alone?'

His answer was to take hold of her waist in both hands; before Caro could do anything to stop him he had lifted her, in spite of her struggles, out of the car.

'I am not going in there!' she shouted at him, glaring up into his face.

'Yes, you are,' he said with every sign of assurance.

'I won't, and you can't make me!'

'Oh, yes, I can,' said Gil with a mocking little smile.

Caro mutinously set her mouth and dug her heels in like a mule, backing towards the car. He still held on to her waist, and she couldn't help registering that his fingers almost touched in the middle because his hands were long and her waist small. She felt a strange flutter of pleasure, conscious of the warmth of his hands pressing in upon her body. It was a possessive hold, a dominating one, and she wanted to yield to it.

'You are an infuriating woman,' Gil observed, eyeing her as if he disliked her intensely, at which she was fiercely pleased because at least he wasn't ignoring her now, or treating her with drawling amusement.

'You're an infuriating man,' she retorted, and Gil laughed shortly.

'And you've always got an answer, haven't you?'

'If you mean I won't let you bully me and get away with it, then yes!' she said, very aware of the warm darkness around them, their isolation in the quiet street.

And then behind Caro the front door opened, a beam of yellow light cut the darkness on the driveway and no doubt illumined their figures by the Rolls. Caro stiffened, wondering if this was Lady Westbrook—or was it the Countess coming out to welcome Gil home, unaware that he was not alone? She had no time to turn her head to find out, because Gil bent suddenly and took her mouth in a hot, urgent kiss.

CHAPTER FIVE

CARO was so startled and taken aback that she didn't even have the strength of mind to push him away or slap his face, although afterwards she wished she had—not that Gil gave her the opportunity of doing anything.

He took her mouth ruthlessly; his hands manipulated her, as if she were a doll, pulled her towards him until their bodies touched, his fast-breathing chest rising and and falling against her own, his thigh pushing intimately between hers. His mouth was torment and enchantment; she met the invasion helplessly, her eyes closing, plunging her into hot darkness where nothing mattered but the sweetness of that kiss, her lips parting weakly to kiss him back.

When Gil at last lifted his head again she was so feverish she shivered, still clinging to his shoulders in case her legs gave way and she fell at his feet, the way she had that first time they had ever met. She was angry, too, wanted to shout at him, hit him, because he was using her, somehow, kissing her deliberately as part of some plan—but what, and why? That was what puzzled her.

Then Gil turned towards the door, gave a rather overdone start of surprise and said blandly, 'Why, hello, Miranda! What are you doing here?'

Then Caro knew, of course. He had kissed her to annoy the Countess; perhaps they had quarrelled? Or he liked to make Miranda jealous? Whatever the reason, it had all been a game, with Caro used as a pawn, and her throat went tight with pain and resentment.

The slender blonde gave him an over-brilliant smile, as shiny as the diamonds she wore around her throat and on her ears. From her expression, Gil had achieved his aim: Miranda was furious. 'I've been trying to get you on the phone, Gil darling, but you weren't at your office, or your home, so I rang your grandmother's house and she very sweetly invited me to dinner. She said you were coming, and we've been waiting for you for ages. Your grandmother is quite cross with you for being so late.' She didn't seem to have noticed he was not alone; Caro could have been invisible for all the notice the Countess took of her.

Caro wasn't hanging around to be humiliated or cold-shouldered; she turned blindly to start walking home; it was only a short distance round the corner, after all. She only took one step before Gil's arm caught her waist and drew her close again.

'Miranda, I don't think you've met Caroline Ramsgate, have you?' he drawled. 'Caroline, this is the Countess of Jurby.'

The two young women regarded each other as if from opposite ends of the earth. Neither smiled or moved.

Gil Martell looked amused; Caro could have kicked him. Lightly, he said, 'I'm sure my grandmother has mentioned that Caroline's father may be taking over Westbrooks.'

Miranda's perfectly pencilled brows arched. 'Oh, she's that man's daughter, is she? I see.' Her voice held oceans of meaning and Caro hated her smile. 'Well, we must be terribly nice to her, mustn't we?'

'Caro is having dinner too,' Gil said and Miranda's smile hardened.

'Your grandmother didn't mention that.'

Caro opened her mouth to say she was not having dinner, she was going home, but Gil forestalled her, steering her firmly towards the open front door where they were met by the short, stout woman whom Caro had met on her first visit.

'Oh, hello, Susan,' Gil said casually. 'You remember Caro, don't you? She was here to dinner last week, with her father. I've invited her again—what have you got for us?'

'Oh, dear,' Susan said, biting her lip and looking flustered. 'Nothing special, I'm afraid—just melon and Parma ham, followed by chicken casserole, and then coffee mousse... Really, Gil, I don't know if there will be enough...'

'Sounds delicious,' he said in his ruthless way, throwing her a charming but insistent smile Caro recognised all too well. So he was like that with everyone, not just with her, was he? That ought to make her feel better, but it didn't. 'And I'm sure it will easily stretch to feed five, especially as I'm certain Caro is on a diet.' He gave the maddening smile to Caro. 'Aren't you, Caro? Women usually are. I've never known a woman yet who wasn't, at one time or another.'

Miranda eyed Caro's figure, so much more rounded and richly curved than her own, with a smiling disdain meant for Caro to see, which, of course, she did, angrily flushing.

'Well, of course, I'm sure your grandmother will be delighted to see Miss Ramsgate again, but...if you're sure you don't mind a small portion, Miss Ramsgate...but the mousse is very small,' Susan bleated unhappily, torn between courtesy and truth.

Gil soon disposed of that argument. 'I shall have cheese, not the mousse, so you can give my share of that to Caro. Now, off you go, Susan, and set a place for her, will you?'

Lady Westbrook's companion-housekeeper vanished to obey without another word, used, no doubt, to being given such arrogant commands, and Gil propelled Caro through the hall and into the drawing-room she remembered all too clearly, her eyes rapidly flickering round the high-ceilinged room with its tapestry-upholstered Victorian furniture and faded, richly coloured carpets. Lady Westbrook was seated beside a fire which had been lit, although spring had now begun. She stared across the room at Caro in startled surprise, and Caro gave her a shy, uncertain smile, lost for words.

'Caro has been working in my office so hard all day,' Gil smoothly explained. 'She was looking tired, so I brought her home to dinner.'

Lady Westbrook courteously extended a hand. 'Well, I'm so glad, how nice to see you again, Caroline. I hope Gilham has been giving you everything you need?'

'I've tried my best,' purred Gil, grinning like a Cheshire cat.

'Good,' said his grandmother, innocently unaware of the wicked double meaning of his tone or the teasing glint in the dark eyes. Fortunately, she seemed equally blind to Caro's flushed cheeks, and, pointing to a chair, said, 'Bring that over here, Gil, so that Caroline can come and sit by me, and tell me how her investigation is coming along. Or aren't I supposed to ask that?'

'It's early days yet,' Caro said, furiously glaring at Gil as he carried the chair and put it down next to his grandmother. 'It takes quite a time to get out a full report on a company.'

Miranda was staring, her face puzzled. 'A report on what?' she asked Caro, who did not answer, just looked in Gil's direction, leaving it to him to explain to Miranda.

'Caro's an accountant,' Gil said.

'An accountant?' repeated Miranda, looking down her long, aristocratic nose in disbelief and hauteur. 'A woman accountant?' She made it sound bizarre, incredible. Gil laughed; Caro did not.

'Why not?' she coldly asked. 'Men no longer monopolise the professions, you know. Weren't you a model, years ago, before you got married?'

Miranda did not like the way she had put that. Her eyes glittered. 'I only gave up work two years ago!' she snapped.

Caro shrugged indifferently. 'Well, my point is that at one time women had very few choices of career. Teaching, nursing, acting, modelling, office work—that was about it for women, but these days things are very different. A woman can do any job; all that matters is her ability.'

'Even so, I doubt if many women opt for accountancy, rather than being a model!' drawled Gil, and Miranda laughed softly.

'I couldn't agree more, darling.'

Lady Westbrook cut across this conversation to ask, 'How is your father, Caroline?'

'He's always well,' Caro answered with a wry little smile. 'I can't remember him ever being ill. An occasional cold, perhaps, but nothing worse.'

Susan hurried into the room, looking agitated. 'Dinner is ready now,' she breathlessly told them, and Gil came to help his grandmother to her feet, then took her arm to lead her off to dinner. Caro watched them thoughtfully. They might be at odds at the moment, Lady

Westbrook might plan to sell the store over his head, but it was very clear that Gil was strongly attached to his grandmother, and that she, however angry with him she might be at the moment, loved him dearly.

Caro frowned. In that case, how serious was this split between them? Would the old lady really go through with her sale of Westbrooks?

Over dinner Miranda tried to monopolise Gil's attention, flirting with him, eyes huge and apparently magnetic, smile deliberately alluring, while she ignored Caro, who sat there in silence, eating very little and wishing she were somewhere else. Why had she let him talk her into staying for dinner? She must be out of her mind. Why had he wanted her there? And how serious was his relationship with the lovely Countess?

'I'm staying at the Savoy,' Miranda murmured, her hand lightly brushing Gil's as he refilled her wine glass with some of the light, delicious white wine being served with the chicken. He gave her a frowning look and she fluttered her lashes. 'Well, you told me to choose neutral ground, darling, so I have—a hotel is as neutral as anywhere, wouldn't you say? I left a message at the Hall telling Colin where I was, so he can't say he doesn't know. I've taken a suite—well, why not? I might as well be comfortable, and the windows look out over the Thames through all those lovely new leaves on the trees. London is simply magical in spring, isn't it? I always think it such a green city. The bed in my suite is a four-poster, with the most gorgeous brocade curtains I've seen in ages. You'll love them.'

Lady Westbrook sat up stiffly in her chair, her eyes round with shocked consternation. 'What do you mean, Miranda? Have you left your husband?'

'Yes, I'm afraid I have. Well, what else could I do? After he made that terrible scene in public!' Miranda turned wide-open, innocent eyes on her, but Lady Westbrook was not to be softened.

'You don't have to make matters worse by leaving him!' she snapped.

'You don't know what you're talking about! Gil knows what I've had to put up with from Colin! Ask him! This isn't the first time my husband has embarrassed me in front of all my friends, but it's going to be the last!' Miranda's surface sweetness cracked a little and revealed a hardness underneath; no surprise to Caro, or to Lady Westbrook, from her expression.

'I don't think we should talk about this over dinner,' Gil said impatiently, and Miranda let her blonde head droop close to his shoulder, a fragile femininity in the movement.

'Whatever you say, darling.'

Lady Westbrook eyed Miranda with the look of one who was longing to give somebody a smack; in this case, thought Caro, richly deserved. She wouldn't mind giving Miranda a smack herself. Instead, she ate her small portion of coffee mousse, her eyes riveted on her plate.

The food was good, what there was of it; meant obviously for three, it barely ran to five, and everyone had cheese after the sweet. There was an excellent and very large cheeseboard, and after that they retired to the drawing-room to have their coffee, carried there by Susan on a silver tray which seemed much too heavy for her.

Gil leapt to take it from her as she staggered in with it. 'Sit down, Susan,' he ordered in his peremptory way. 'I'll pour it out. You must be exhausted, after cooking that wonderful meal for us—you're a marvellous cook, were you trained at college? Or did you just pick it up?'

'Oh...thank you... I...I did a cookery course, years ago, yes, but I've learnt far more by just practising, finding out what works and what doesn't.' Susan sat down, bright pink with pleasure, while Gil lifted the massive silver coffee-pot and began to pour fragrant dark coffee into the small bone china cups, so fragile they were actually transparent; Caro could see the whorled pads of his fingers through them.

She watched him intently, absorbing his kindness to his grandmother's companion, his awareness of the work she had done, and the way he took care to thank Susan for it. Like his tenderness and affection for his grandmother, this was another aspect of his character that she was discovering. She was surprised by it—although why should she be? she asked herself. No man was one-dimensional, they were all layered, and Gil Martell was particularly complex, she was realising.

They were drinking their coffee when the doorbell rang violently. Susan shot to her feet, almost dropping her coffee-cup. Miranda stiffened in her chair, her blue eyes wide. 'Colin!'

'What on earth makes you think it's your husband?' asked Lady Westbrook impatiently, and Gil slowly stood up, staring at Miranda.

'If you left word that you were at the Savoy, why would he come here?' he asked in sharp suspicion.

'I don't know...don't you start bullying me!' wailed Miranda, and Caro might have been sympathetic if she hadn't been convinced that that look of terror was too theatrical to be true. Miranda was enjoying herself too much to be genuinely afraid.

Gil did not seem impressed, either. 'What have you been up to, Miranda?' he asked. 'You told him you were coming here tonight, didn't you?'

She pushed out her lower lip in what she no doubt hoped would be a childishly appealing pout, and looked reproachfully at Gil. 'I didn't tell Colin anything. But if he rang the Savoy...' Her voice trailed off and Gil grimaced.

'You left a message with them that you would be here. I see.'

'My mother might have rung! She said she was going to!' Miranda defended herself.

The ringing came again, louder and more peremptory.

'Susan, answer the door,' Lady Westbrook ordered, and her companion with obvious reluctance crept away to obey.

'No, don't,' Miranda burst out, and Susan stopped in the doorway, looking back at her employer.

'Do as I say!' snapped Lady Westbrook, and Susan hurried off.

Miranda groaned. 'Oh, don't let him in, Lady Westbrook—you don't know how he can be in one of his jealous moods, especially if he's been drinking, and at this time of the evening he will have been drinking, he has probably spent hours at his club, in the bar.'

From the hall came loud voices—a man's deep, angry tones and Susan's high, anxious ones. Gil strode towards the door, frowning, but before he got there it was flung open and another man appeared, throwing a surly look around the drawing-room.

Caro vaguely remembered the face from that photograph which had appeared in the newspapers. The Earl of Jurby was a little older than Gil Martell, a man of around forty, with a long, rather plain face, darkly flushed at present and full of aggression, although his features were quite pleasant and in other moods he was possibly very likeable.

His eye lighted on Gil, and he glared at him, baring his teeth. 'Oh, there you are! That silly woman who opened the door kept trying to tell me you weren't here. I knew she was lying. Where's my wife, you swine?'

'Colin, you're drunk...' Gil began, but the other man caught sight of Miranda on the other side of the room and snarled triumphantly.

'So she is here! I knew it, I knew I'd find her with you! That message she left about dining with your grandmother didn't fool me for a minute!' He lurched towards Gil, his hands screwed into fists, a strange, dishevelled sight in the elegant drawing-room, his reddish hair windblown, his tie undone and his shirt-collar open at the throat. 'I'm going to kill you, Martell.'

Lady Westbrook's icy voice cracked like a whip. 'How dare you behave like this in my house? Where are your manners, sir? This is my drawing-room, not a bar-room!'

The Earl halted, stiffened, turning scarlet, and peered across the room at her, swaying unsteadily from side to side. 'Good lord! Gil, your grandmother is here. Thought it was all a lie, made a mistake... apologise, Lady W...' He ran a hand over his brow, thinking. 'Lady Westbrook,' he triumphantly remembered. 'I beg your pardon. Terrible manners. Absolutely. No excuse. One drink too many.' He bowed, almost fell over, and Gil grabbed his arm and hauled him upright again.

'Thanks, Gil,' he automatically said, beginning to make his slow, ponderous way to the door like a short-sighted elephant, then paused again, looked round helplessly. 'Wasn't my wife here? Oh, there she is...Miranda...you might give a fellow a helping hand,' he said pathetically.

'Oh, go home, Colin!' she snapped, her face angrily flushed.

'Well, I shall, but where's my car? Did I come here in my car?' He stopped to think, shook his head. 'No, took a taxi. Someone at the club said . . . no, policeman said . . . in no state to drive, took my keys away.'

'That's true enough, heaven knows,' Gil said tersely. 'I'll drive him home, shall I, Miranda?'

The Earl petulantly pushed him away. 'Don't want you to drive me, Gilham. My wife can drive.'

'Why should I?' Miranda crossly asked him. 'Just look at you! You've been drinking again and I'm sick of living with someone who sees the world through the bottom of a glass. Take a taxi home, Colin. Walk. Sleep on a park bench! I don't care what you do, but I'm not going back home with you.'

'Miranda, darling, don't be nasty to me!' he mumbled, trying to put an arm round her, and she pushed him away.

'Leave me alone!'

'I think you should have this discussion somewhere else,' Gil said, seeing the anger in his grandmother's face. 'Miranda, help me get Colin into the hall. Come on, Colin, don't be an idiot . . . you can't talk to Miranda in here.' He jerked his head towards his grandmother, and the Earl looked blankly at her, then gave a loud gasp.

'Oh, quite . . . Sorry . . . leave immediately . . .'

'This way,' Gil drily said, propelling him through the door. The Countess reluctantly followed; the door closed on all three, and Lady Westbrook let out a long, audible breath. Caro felt intense relief, too, and sighed, which brought the old lady's eyes round to her face. Lady Westbrook frowned then, as if only just remembering her presence.

'I apologise, Caroline,' she said stiffly.

'No, please...really...it doesn't matter,' stammered Caro, wishing she was somewhere else.

'It does indeed!' Lady Westbrook said sternly. 'My grandson is behaving disgracefully, and I'm sorry you had to be a witness to that unpleasant little scene. He had no business allowing it to take place in front of you.'

Caro suddenly saw that the old lady's hands were shaking violently, and felt a pang of sympathy. She got up and went over to Lady Westbrook, knelt down beside her chair and took hold of her trembling hands. Their skin was dry and papery, very cold. Caro massaged them gently, smiling into the pale old face.

'Don't upset yourself, it isn't worth it.'

There was the gleam of tears in Lady Westbrook's eyes. Her mouth quivered. 'He's such a fool!'

'Gil?' guessed Caro. She wouldn't argue with that; he was undoubtedly a fool, getting involvd with a woman like Miranda.

'I warned him Miranda meant trouble,' Lady Westbrook muttered, as if reading Caro's thoughts. 'I know the type. Easily bored, always looking for new sensations, extravagant...if Colin divorces her Gil will have to marry her, and she'll ruin his life. My family worked very hard to build up our business, and I'd rather leave the money to charity than let it fall into Miranda's hands and have her spend it all on herself.'

'Is that why you're selling Westbrooks?' asked Caro gently and Lady Westbrook gave her a strange look, half angry, half miserable.

She nodded, then bit her lip before bursting out, 'I gave him an ultimatum. He either swore never to see Miranda again there and then—or I would offer the store to your father!'

Caro whistled softly, imagining the scene. She knew Gil Martell by now; she knew how he would react to that piece of blackmail. His grandmother should have known, too. Her grey eyes gazed at Lady Westbrook, who stared down into them defiantly.

'Oh, I know what you're thinking! It was a mistake, I knew it the minute I'd said it, but I was so angry, and Gil wouldn't talk about it, he just told me to mind my own business! I lost my temper, and I'd said it before I could stop myself, and...and...'

'And he told you to do as you liked, he didn't give a damn?' Caro could almost hear him saying it. She began to laugh and Lady Westbrook stared at her in utter amazement for a minute, and then suddenly she began to laugh, too, the tears still in her eyes.

When their laughter died away the old lady produced a handkerchief and dried her eyes, and gave Caro a shaky smile. 'Thank you for listening, my dear, you're very kind.'

'Not at all.' Caro was shy now; she didn't know what to say or do.

A French clock on the mantelshelf chimed musically, and she started, looking at her own watch in surprise and relief. It was a way out.

'Gracious, look at the time! It is nearly ten o'clock. I'd no idea it was so late. I must be going. Thank you so much for the delicious meal, I enjoyed seeing you again, getting to know you better.'

She was gabbling, she thought; gabbling, no other word for it. Tonight had been quite an ordeal; she had never in her life had to face anything like it. She had been flung from one emotional situation to another all evening, and she was mentally drained. It wasn't over yet, either. To leave, she had to make her way across

that hall, where no doubt there was still a nasty tri-
angular scene going on. She wished there was some other
way out, but she couldn't stay here a second longer, she
had to get away.

'But you must wait for Gil to come back!' Lady
Westbrook protested.

Not on your life! thought Caro, but could not say
that, so instead she muttered, 'Oh, I'll see him on my
way out, I expect.'

'But how will you get home?'

'Our house is just five minutes away, I'll walk.'

'In the dark? I don't think you should, my dear,' Lady
Westbrook argued unhappily, but Caro shook hands and
bolted out of the room.

For a second she thought the hall was empty, and then
she heard the slam of the great oak front door and Gil
moved towards her from the shadows around it. He
halted as he saw her, lifting his dark brows.

'Where are you going?'

'Home,' she said tersely.

He didn't argue. 'I'll drive you,' he said, turning to
walk beside her as she purposefully made for the front
door.

'No, thanks. I prefer to walk,' she said, coolly. 'Good
for the digestion.'

'Then I'll walk you home,' he said at once.

'There's no need...' she protested.

'I can't let you leave here alone at this hour. If anything happened to you, your father would want my
blood.' Gil waved her through the open door into the
cloudless, spring night. It was so clear that you could
almost count the stars, and a bright silvery moon hung
low over London's crowded streets. 'A lovely night,' Gil
murmured, closing the door behind them both.

Caro began to walk, uneasily aware of him walking at her side. Their footsteps rang crisply on the pavements, and above that noise she heard the rustling of the wind in the trees in the darkened park.

Even the traffic was hushed at this hour; few cars came through these very exclusive streets at night. There were lighted windows in some houses, but few sounds. They might have been alone on a desert island and she walked faster, wanting to get home, to get away from his disturbing presence.

Gil looked sideways at her profile as they walked under a street lamp and were illumined to each other by the hazy circle of yellowish light. She was aware of his scrutiny, but didn't show as much, her lashes down against her cheeks and her mouth obstinate.

'OK, say it,' he suddenly said and the sharp note in his voice made her jump.

'Say what?'

They had walked on into the shadows again, and they had almost reached her home—she could see the garden trees, the chalice-like, ivory tipped with pink buds of the magnolia, ghostly and enchanting in moonlight.

'Do you think I wasn't aware what you were thinking?' Gil ground out, halting in his tracks and seizing her arm to swing her round to face him. 'You've been giving off waves of disapproval all evening. I'm beginning to recognise that look, you little prude! You can stop it right now! Miranda has gone back to her husband—I hope that's OK with you?'

'She's gone back home?' Caro said huskily, her eyes clearing, and Gil glared at her, his fingers biting into her arm.

'That's right. Happy now?'

'Obviously you're not,' she muttered. 'And you're hurting my arm! Will you let go of me?'

He released her arm, but, when she tried to walk on, stepped into her path, blocking her way and radiating threat.

'How I feel about Miranda and Colin is my business, not yours. You don't know anything about me, or them and——' He broke off, breathing fiercely, staring down at her. 'You have a maddening way of staring at people and looking superior, do you know that? Stop it! What do you think gives you the right to sit in judgement on me?'

'You're a mind-reader, are you?' Caro muttered, eyeing him with dislike. 'Well, I hope you're reading my mind now. It will save me the trouble of telling you what I think of you!'

She pushed him away, using all her strength, and took him so much by surprise that he lost his balance and floundered back into a hedge. Caro didn't wait to see if he was hurt; she started to run, and reached the driveway of her home before Gil caught up with her. He launched himself at her in a rugby tackle, grabbing her shoulders with both hands and knocking her sideways.

She reeled backwards until she hit a tree trunk and could go no further.

'Get your hands off me!' she whispered, her breathing rapid after running so hard. 'Are you crazy? Chasing me along the street——'

'That was what I was meant to do, wasn't it?' he said, his mouth a cynical curve. 'You ran, expecting me to run after you.'

'No!' she denied, but felt a strange confusion—that wasn't what she had wanted, was it? For him to follow, catch her?

Gil smiled crookedly. 'Sure about that? People talk about men being primitive—but it's women who have the primitive instincts; they love to run away and have men chasing after them.'

'If that's your excuse, you can forget it!' Caro hated the way he was smiling. 'I certainly don't want you chasing me. Your lady-friend may enjoy being chased, she may like to play primitive games, but I don't!'

She shouldn't have brought Miranda into it again; it made him angrier. His face tightened, his skin dark.

'That's enough!' he snapped, holding her against the tree, his grip unbreakable. 'Why are you so obsessed with Miranda, anyway? You get in digs about her whenever you get the chance. I'd almost think you were jealous of her!'

Caro went scarlet, her whole body reacting in shock. She was appalled, yet she couldn't get out a single word to deny it.

Gil's eyes had narrowed and he was watching her intently now, trying to read her expression. 'You can't be jealous over me, we've only just met,' he said slowly. 'Why should you dislike Miranda so much? Because she's a famous beauty? Because men flock around her?' His mouth twisted in distaste. 'Women are the most extraordinary creatures. You envy Miranda, yet you give off that puritanical air, as if you've never been to bed with a man in your life.'

Caro's face was burning, and his dark eyes glittered. 'Did I hit a nail on the head?'

Caro was so angry her voice sounded high and shaky. 'No, you didn't!'

'You mean you have been to bed with a man?' he mockingly enquired, and she was too humiliated to care what she said any more.

'I'm not as promiscuous as you and your women, anyway! You may think nothing of leaping in and out of bed with anyone you happen to meet, whether they're married to someone else, or not—but I prefer to keep a little self-respect!'

Gil's crooked smile vanished; he looked at her with a fury that made her nerves jump. 'You little——' he began thickly, then broke off, breathing roughly. There was a long, tense silence; Caro was dry-mouthed and dumb, her ears beating with the sound of her own blood. She wasn't quite sure what was going to happen next, only that they were locked in what felt like mortal combat. When he moved her whole body jerked in apprehension, as if expecting a blow, but he didn't strike her. He kissed her—if you could call it a kiss.

His mouth hit hers like a weapon, forcing her head back against the tree so that her throat was stretched tight, her lips burnt and aching, her eyes wide and hot with unshed tears. It seemed a long, long time before he stopped and then he straightened up and stood there, breathing as if it hurt him, his eyes shut, his lids like the carved eye-sockets of a stone figure.

Caro didn't move, either; she was crying silently, tears trickling down her white cheeks.

Gil opened his eyes at last and looked at her, his brows jerking together as he saw her face. He swore under his breath. 'I'm sorry. God knows what came over me. I lost my temper. It all got out of hand.'

She couldn't stop crying, partly because she was in shock, and partly because her mouth was swollen and hot, as if she had been stung by a bee.

He groaned. 'Caro, please! Don't!' he said, raking his hands through his thick black hair. 'What on earth can I say to you? I didn't mean that to happen.'

That made it worse; that was terrible. Gil hadn't wanted to kiss her at all, he had done it out of sheer temper, and now he wished he hadn't. She hated him and, at the same time, she cried helplessly.

Gil suddenly bent his head; his mouth brushed her lids, and that was comforting; she sighed shudderingly. It sent a shock of disbelief through her a second later, though, when she felt the tip of his tongue run along her wet lashes. Her sobs stopped, she stood very still, quivering at the strange sensation, her tears over.

'That's better,' he whispered, dropping brief, light kisses on her brow, her eyes, cheeks, nose. He put both arms around her and began to rock her on his body, murmuring soothingly to her as if she were a child, stroking her long brown hair, holding her close.

Now that they had both calmed down, she could have escaped, pushed him away, run up the drive into her house, but she didn't; she leaned on him, letting the warmth of his body seep into her, and after a while he put a finger under her chin to lift her head and kissed her again, very differently, his lips gentle, sensual, their caress making a languorous sweetness grow inside her body. Her arms went round his neck; she kissed him back, her hands in his thick dark hair, becoming aware of a tension in the muscles at the back of his neck and gently massaging it away.

He groaned, lifting his mouth. 'Mmm...that's nice. Don't stop. I've had the most appalling day, just one damn thing after another—that's just what I need.' He buried his face in her throat, and one hand strokingly explored her body in the tight-fitting jersey wool dress.

Alarm bells began to ring inside her head a second later as she felt the long zip unpeel down the back of her dress and Gil's hand slide inside.

'I must go in,' she stammered, hearing the thud of his heart close to her, the rough sound of his breathing.

'Not yet,' he said, and she watched his mouth and ached with desire, but she had herself under control now; she was able to think clearly again. What was in Gil's mind? No prizes for guessing that. He was making it pretty obvious. His hand had moved silkily round to her breasts; she tightened in panic as his fingers intimately caressed her bare, warm skin. She had to stop him before it was too late.

She didn't kid herself that it was really her Gil wanted. He would have made a pass at any woman who happened to come along tonight. Gil had just had to watch his lover go back to her husband, and he was angry, jealous, unhappy.

He needed some comfort, he needed to feel somebody wanted him, he needed a woman; but Caro wasn't prepared to accept the role. Briefly, she had felt such a wild pull of attraction that she might have been fool enough to let him go on making love to her, but she had waited too long to fall in love to be ready to play stand-in to some other woman.

When a man made love to her, it was going to be because he loved and wanted her, herself, and not for any other reason.

She pushed Gil away with such force that he went in sheer surprise. 'No,' she said sharply.

He blinked, suddenly shaken out of that physical absorption in pleasure. 'What's wrong?'

'I don't want to get involved,' Caro said. 'Please, stop it. I'm tired, no doubt you are, it has been a very long day. Can we just say goodnight?'

The heated excitement drained slowly out of Gil's face as he met her cool stare. 'I didn't have you down as a tease!' he muttered, then dropped his hands and shrugged. 'Oh, have it your own way, then! Goodnight!'

Caro didn't hang about to be polite. She wanted to put as much space between them as she could, so now that she was free she just ran, without looking back. All the same, she felt his anger following her every step of the way.

CHAPTER SIX

CARO went in to work next morning so nervous that she twice changed her clothes before deciding to wear a straight black skirt and white V-necked sweater. It wasn't exactly eye-catching, but it made the most of her figure without being too obvious about it. She brushed her brown hair slowly in front of the mirror, gloomily eyeing her face and wishing she was prettier. What was the point of wishing, though? Men didn't turn to stare at her in the street, and that was that. She could spend hours doing her make-up, clip pearl earrings into her ears, fuss over her clothes—but it wouldn't make any difference. She had no glamour, and that was something the Countess of Jurby had in abundance.

There were butterflies in her stomach when she walked out of the lift and into Gil's office. His secretary looked up at her entrance and gave a brief nod. She still wasn't any friendlier, but Caro was used to her hostility by now.

There was no sign of Gil himself, thank heavens. Caro knew he would spend most of the morning on his tour of the store, but although she expected that, the morning dragged by; Caro kept watching the clock but the more she watched, the slower the hands seemed to move. Gil didn't appear until almost lunchtime and, when he did arrive, had two senior members of his staff with him. They walked in talking, Gil wearing one of his beautifully tailored formal suits, a dark blue pin-stripe, with which he wore a crisp white shirt and blue silk tie.

He looked striking, and Caro was angry with herself for feeling an immediate stab of pleasure so sharp it was almost pain. What he felt, she could not guess from his expression. He nodded curtly, but didn't say anything, walked behind her desk and paused for a moment to observe what she was doing, then, still without a word, went back to his own desk, collected some documents from a locked drawer and walked out again, his employees following.

Stupidly, she felt as if he had slapped her in the face. He might have said something! A few polite words wouldn't have hurt him, would they? She forced herself back to work, but found it hard to concentrate.

Gil came back at seven minutes to three that afternoon. Caro knew what time it was because she kept looking at the clock and wondering, Where is he? She looked up as he walked in, tensing, but he still didn't say anything. She watched the hard outline of his profile, her throat dry with nerves. Just having him in the same room had become both an ordeal and a painful delight. His secretary walked into the office and Gil gestured to the chair in front of his desk. He smiled at the woman; Caro watched through her lashes and ached with stupid, pointless jealousy. He had no smiles for her, it seemed. He had become quite friendly for a little while; now they were back to the cold war, and Caro hated it.

He spent the next hour dictating to his secretary, then left again, without even glancing in Caro's direction. She understood. He regretted making love to her last night; he didn't want her to think it had meant anything. He was staying out of her way and treating her remotely so that she shouldn't be under any illusion about their relationship. Her father's intention of buying Westbrooks made them enemies. Well, he needn't bother to hammer home the point.

She had known, last night, just why he had been kissing her. That was why she had stopped him. Last night, Gil had been walking a knife-edge of anger and frustration. Of course, he should never have got involved with a married woman, but he must be unhappy, and Caro hated the thought of him...of anyone...being unhappy.

But being unhappy didn't give him the right to treat other people so ruthlessly.

He had kissed her and tried to make love to her without caring how she might feel. He had tried to take advantage of her—and now, no doubt, he was afraid that she might try to take advantage of him! What did he think she might do? Tell Miranda? Or perhaps his grandmother?

Caro stared at the window, seeing nothing of the London roofs, the blue spring sky it framed. Were all men opportunists, not to be trusted? Wasn't there one of the sex that you could rely on?

Gil's secretary came in to say coldly that she was now leaving, and reminded Caro about the time when the security staff would want her out of the building.

'I'm going now,' Caro said irritably, getting up.

Amy rang her that evening, bubbling over with excitement. 'You remember Antony Calthrop?'

'No,' Caro said, half yawning.

'Yes, you do, darling,' insisted Amy.

'No, I don't,' said Caro, to whom the name was totally unknown.

'You do, he's a surgeon, ear, nose and throat ops, at St Luke's Hospital. He took my tonsils out last year. Tall guy, lanky, hair sort of straw-coloured. He isn't good-looking, exactly, but he has a terrific bedside manner.'

Caro gave a burst of laughter. 'I see! He's your latest, is he?'

'No, darling,' protested Amy. 'No, the point is ... he's giving a flat-warming party, he just moved to St John's Wood, to be nearer the hospital, and he's invited me.'

'Wonderful, have a great time. Tell me all about it when we have lunch.' Caro was eager to have a bath, wallow in her misery, and then go to bed to wallow some more. The last thing she wanted was to talk about men. They were not her favourite subject at the moment.

'Hang on,' Amy said hurriedly. 'Caro, he remembered meeting you at the hospital when you visited me.'

'Well, I don't remember meeting him. It was over a year ago!' Caro couldn't actually remember much about her visit to see Amy except that her friend could only eat jelly and ice-cream and had kept whispering mournfully that her throat hurt. Fred Ramsgate had come along too, because Amy was one of his favourite people, and he had been very anxious about her.

'Oh, don't tell him that,' said Amy, sounding horrified. 'It will hurt his feelings. I said I was sure you remembered him, he had made a big impression on you ...'

'Oh, did you?' said Caro indignantly.

Amy gave one of her little giggles. 'Well, he is so sweet, I was sure he must have done! He was delighted to hear you remembered him so well——'

'Oh, really, Amy!'

'So he invited you to the party!'

'What?' Caro exclaimed, appalled. 'I can't go, thanks all the same, Amy. Very kind of him, but I'm busy that night.'

'I haven't told you when it is yet!'

'Whenever it is, I am busy. I'm not being dragged off on one of your famous blind dates. Every time you meet a man who is too ghastly for words you kindly decide to land me with him, while you go off with the only good-looking guy in sight.'

'Antony isn't ghastly,' protested Amy. 'Honestly, darling, he isn't, he's funny and kind and sweet, and you'll love him.'

'I doubt that,' Caro said grimly. 'If he's so gorgeous, why aren't you dating him?'

Amy giggled. 'I'm going with someone else, or I would. Look, darling, if you really don't like Antony, it won't matter because he's invited hordes of people. He's the host, so he'll be kept busy... you know how it is at a party. You don't have to stay, but do come, or he'll be furious with me for taking another man to his party.'

'You're totally ruthless, aren't you?' Caro didn't know whether to laugh or be shocked. If her father could hear Amy now! His image of her as a sweetly feminine creature would be blown to smithereens.

Amy laughed, quite flattered by the comment. 'We'll call for you at eight next Saturday,' she said. 'Antony's new flat is only on the other side of the park from your house, Rob says.'

'Rob? That's the newest heart-throb, is it?' asked Caro, but Amy just giggled and rang off. Caro hung up, too, her eyes thoughtful. Perhaps, this time, Amy was serious about someone? She wasn't usually so secretive about her men; she usually talked about them non-stop. Caro was curious about the unknown Rob.

Well, a party would make a change, and might even cheer her up, she ruefully decided, and went off to look through her wardrobe and choose something special to wear.

By the end of the following week, all the work on the Westbrooks accounts was finished, and her team had completed their detailed analysis, with the usual set of graphs suggesting future growth and areas of change, and corresponding graphs making clear the necessity to clear away dead wood and stop wastage. Caro saw to it that just enough copies were printed out for her father and the rest of his board, and then removed the master tape.

She did not want any copies falling into the wrong hands. Anyone who saw that report and could understand its significance could make a killing on the stock market before the Westbrooks sale went ahead.

Gil had been in and out of his office over the last few days, and he, for one, would love to see that report. If she had not removed the master tape and taken it away with her each night, she was sure he would have come in early one morning and managed to break into her computer to check over the material. Of course, all the originating accounts were his; but it was her conclusions Gil wanted to read. He knew everything there was to know about the way Westbrooks was running—what he was dying to know was, what did Caro think of the store's financial condition? And what were her plans for the future, should her company take over the store?

Her father read her report that Friday evening, after dinner, and sat up until the small hours with it in his study while Caro went to bed early. When she got up next morning, she found him at the breakfast table, heavy-lidded and yawning over his boiled eggs and toast.

'Late night?' she asked, pouring herself coffee.

He grunted, pushing his own cup towards her. 'I was up reading that tome of yours! I must say, you did the job thoroughly.'

'Thank you,' she said, smiling. It was always nice to be praised for work well done.

'I just had a few queries,' Fred said, pushing a pile of notes towards her.

She viewed them with wary amusement. 'A few?'

'One or two points that needed clarifying,' he amended as she picked up the sheaf of paper and glanced through it, groaning.

'Dad, this means going back to Westbrooks and putting in at least two or three hours' work! I thought I'd finished with the place.' And with Gil Martell, she thought grimly.

'I'm sorry, love, but it's essential that we have the answers to those points before the board meeting on Monday. Could you pop in there this morning? I'm sure it won't take you long. You're so efficient.'

She gave him a grimacing smile. 'Very flattering, Dad—if I didn't know you were just saying it to get me to do what you want!'

'Nay, love,' he said in his broadest North Country accent, grinning at her. 'As if I'd lie to you! Nay, you're smarter than a whip, and I'm that proud of you!'

She had to laugh at that, and to shrug in resignation. 'OK, I'll go! That's my Saturday at the club gone!' She had intended to do a number of things that morning, and play squash, with friends, at the local sports club on the edge of the park. She knew quite a few of the members; Saturday was the day most of them spent there. After squash they would swim for a while before having a light salad lunch in the poolside bar, and then have their hair styled by the club hairdresser. Caro enjoyed her Saturday mornings at the club. Some members visited it every day; it was the perfect place to meet clients and friends in a relaxed, social atmosphere. She was sorry not to be able to go, after all. Oh, well, she thought. She would just have to ring the club and make her excuses. She wasn't going to be popular with the friends she had been going to meet, but they were all busy working women, they would understand she had had no alternative but to let them down.

By nine-thirty she was back at the desk in Gil's office, working intently, when he strode into the room, black-browed and vibrating with rage.

'They told me you were here! I thought you had finished with our accounts? We showed you everything you asked to see, heaven knows! We didn't hide anything, so why are you back here again?'

Caro fought to hide the confusion she felt at the sight of him; he was dressed more casually than usually, in an old sheepskin, a red sweater and cord trousers. He looked as if he had just been about to go for a walk with his dog, or practise golf shots informally. Had he been at home when the accounts department rang to say she had asked to see the books again? It couldn't have been his secretary because she wasn't around this morning; obviously she had Saturdays off. Where had Gil been? At home? Didn't he work on Saturdays either? Caro would have loved to ask him, but she couldn't risk it. He would probably bite her head off.

'My father read my report last night——' she began instead, and Gil interrupted furiously.

'And that's another thing—I allowed you to study all our account books, we were totally open with you, but you didn't let me have a copy of this wonderful report! Every member of your board will see it, but not me!'

'It's confidential,' she stammered nervously, and he snarled at her, dark eyes glittering.

'I'm sure it is! You don't want me to know exactly what value you put on my store. If I guessed that, I might warn my grandmother to ask for a much higher price than your shark of a father intends to offer her!'

She found it nerve-racking to have him looming over her, so she pushed back her chair and got to her feet, confronting him, her chin up. 'My father isn't a shark! He is offering her a very fair price.'

'Well, you would say that, wouldn't you? After all, he trained you—you're just like him, as predatory, in your own way, as he is!'

She flushed scarlet, so angry that her hand shot out to slap him round the face, but Gil was too quick for her. He caught her wrist, pulling her arm down and at the same time jerking her forward until their bodies touched. An electric shock went through her and for a moment she couldn't breathe.

'Oh, no, you don't!' he ground out. 'No woman hits me!'

Her breathing started again, but it was painfully fast; she couldn't bear being so close to him. 'Why did you insult me, then?' she whispered huskily. 'Do you think you can say what you like to me?'

He frowned, staring down at her. 'I lost my temper...'

'You're always losing your temper!'

'Only around you,' he said, oddly, and she looked up into his eyes, startled by something in his voice. Why was he looking at her like that? Her ears pounded with aroused blood; she was so hot, her temperature must have shot sky-high. Something important, something world-shattering, seemed to be happening to her; time stood still, the world stopped spinning.

And then there was the click of the office door opening, and a voice said, 'Hello? Oh...sorry...am I interrupting anything?' And there was an all too familiar giggle.

Amy! thought Caro dazedly, still staring up into Gil's face. That is Amy. What is she doing here? For an instant, she even thought she was imagining things. How on earth could it be Amy? But just for that second of time she didn't care who it was, she didn't look round, she didn't want anything interrupting her concentration on Gil.

He had ignored the new arrival too; or perhaps he simply hadn't heard a thing. He looked as dazed as Caro felt, his eyes riveted on her flushed face, as if he was trying to read her thoughts. She stared back at him, trying in her turn to read his expression. She wished she knew what was happening, what he was thinking. Was she going crazy, imagining all of this? Was it nothing but wish-fulfilment? Maybe in a minute she would wake up and find she had been dreaming?

Then she heard that giggle again. It wasn't her imagination; that was Amy and she was wide awake. Gil heard it too, this time—he let go of Caro, his head jerking round; Caro reluctantly turned, too.

It was Amy, all right, tiny, pretty, blue-eyed Amy at her most feminine in a lace-ruffled pink dress which showed off that pocket Venus figure and the blonde hair.

'Hello,' Caro said flatly. What on earth was Amy doing here? She was the last person in the world Caro wanted to see right now. She certainly didn't want Amy meeting Gil, but from the bright-eyed interest Amy was showing in him, that might well be why Amy had come. Caro had been fool enough to confide the fact that she was sharing an office with Gil Martell, and Amy had been dying to meet him ever since she saw that photograph of him in the newspaper. I should have known she would show up to see him sooner or later, Caro thought bleakly. I've known Amy for years; when will I learn?

'I came to see if we could have lunch,' Amy said, her eyes on Gil and smiling her sweetest smile. 'I rang you at home and your father said you were here, so I popped along to find you, and that lovely man on the main door showed me up here.' She gave Gil an appealing look. 'I hope you don't mind me visiting your private office?'

'Of course not,' he said, smiling back indulgently, the way men always did when Amy fluttered her lashes at them.

Caro mumbled an introduction, reluctantly, and Amy held out her hand.

'Caro and I were at school together.'

'What was she like at school?' Gil asked her, sliding Caro a teasing look. 'As bossy as she is now?'

'Bossier,' Amy said, still holding his hand and looking up at him, and Caro wondered why she had ever liked her. How had they stayed friends for so long?

'I had to come into town to buy a new dress for a party I'm going to,' Amy confided to him. 'And I thought...why not meet up with Caro? I thought she might want to buy a new dress too, although she always has such wardrobes full of wonderful clothes, lucky girl! I wish my father owned lots of department stores, but I'm an ordinary working girl, I have to buy my own clothes.'

Ordinary working girl! thought Caro. So that's her new image, is it? She gritted her teeth and stoically watched Gil watching Amy.

'I have too much work to do,' she told Amy. 'Sorry, but I can't spare the time for shopping, or lunch.'

'Oh, poor you,' said Amy without so much as looking in her direction. 'That's all she cares about, you know, work,' she told Gil, who grinned.

'I've noticed. A positive workaholic. Do you think she gets it from her father?'

'Do you mind not talking about me?' Caro crossly asked them, but neither took any notice.

'Oh, he's so sweet, darling Fred! But he is obsessed with work, and Caro's always been the same.'

'Don't tell me she's actually going to this party, too?'

Amy nodded. 'Of course she is! Everyone's going to be there, having great fun. It's the place to be tonight.'

'Then why aren't I invited?' His dark eyes teased and Amy gave one of her breathless little laughs.

'Will you come, if I invite you?'

'Nothing would keep me away! I can't wait to see what Caro is like when she's having fun.' His tone was drily incredulous; he was staring at Caro, his brows curved in mockery, and she wanted to hit him.

Looking away, she stared fixedly at Amy, trying to get over to her that she did not want Gil at this party, but although Amy met her eyes, and understood the silent message, she quickly looked away and went ahead, which was utterly typical of her. Amy might look sweetly yielding, but she always insisted on her own way.

'Great!' she merely said to Gil. 'You're invited, then. Eight o'clock tonight. The address is Flat 3, Park View Apartments, Windermere Street, St John's Wood.'

She watched Gil write all that down in his address book, and explained how he would get there from his own home in Regents Park. 'You won't have any problem finding it. It's the newest building in the street.'

'You're giving this party?' Gil enquired.

'No,' Caro stiffly said. 'She isn't, and I don't think she should hand out invitations to someone else's party.'

'Oh, don't be so dreary, darling,' Amy said, very pink and excited. She knew Caro was furious and was avoiding her stare now, but she didn't care because she was in the all too familiar process of falling for Gil. Caro knew all the signs. She ought to! Amy had been in and out of love ever since Caro met her.

'A friend is,' Amy said, not mentioning that the 'friend' was male, and an old boyfriend who might very well resent her bringing along the latest male to catch her eye. 'But I'm organising the party, so I can invite who I like.'

'Can I have a word in private?' Caro asked her coldly, but Amy beat a hasty retreat to the door.

'Tonight, darling,' she said. 'I must rush, if you aren't coming shopping...'

'Well, I'll see you when you pick me up tonight!' Caro grimly promised her, and Amy looked hunted.

'Take a taxi, will you, darling? We'll be going there early to help get everything ready. See you.'

'Amy!' Caro yelled after her, but she had slammed the door and was to be heard almost running away. Gil laughed softly, and Caro turned a furious glare on him.

'What's so funny?'

'Your expression! What's bothering you? The idea of my coming to this party? What might I see? The efficient Miss Ramsgate actually being human?'

'I'm human, don't worry,' Caro snapped. 'As you'll find out if you keep annoying me!'

He laughed. 'I'm shaking in my shoes!'

'Oh, go away!' she angrily muttered. 'You may have nothing better to do, but I must get this work finished or I'll be here until midnight, and I'll miss the party, not that I feel much like going now.'

'You're going, if I have to come and get you myself,' said Gil. 'In fact, I will. I'll pick you up at seven-thirty.'

'No,' she said, horrified by the very idea of going there with him. 'I don't know when I'll be ready—don't bother, I'll take a taxi.'

'You won't,' he insisted. 'I'll pick you up, and it doesn't matter if you aren't ready, because I would like a chance for a chat with your father.'

'Oh, I might have known! You want to talk him into showing you my report, I suppose? You won't succeed. Dad isn't an easy proposition.'

'Something else you have in common,' Gil drily said, and was gone before she could think of anything to say in reply.

When she warned her father that Gil was calling to take her to the party that evening, Fred looked oddly at her. 'You're seeing a lot of him.'

Caro blushed and then was furious. 'I didn't ask him to the party, Amy did.' She explained how it had happened, adding, 'Amy was dying of curiosity about him. She came to the store in the hope of meeting him.'

Fred looked amused. 'I've a lot of time for Amy, she always does go straight for what she wants. And she's so sweet-tempered with it!'

Caro gave him a derisive look. 'You just don't know Amy!' In the hall a clock chimed, and she groaned. 'It's seven o'clock! I don't have time to get ready for the party now, anyway. I don't think I'll go.'

'You will,' Fred said. 'I want you to stay close to Gil Martell, be charming to him, soften him up. We don't want any trouble from him when we take over.'

Nothing her father had said or done had ever shocked her before, but Caro was shocked then, by the idea of being nice to Gil for such a reason.

'I wouldn't be charming to Gil Martell if my life depended on it!' she said fiercely, scowling; and then she went upstairs and began to get ready for the party.

Gil arrived promptly; she heard the doorbell and then the sound of her father being very friendly. Caro grimaced at herself in the mirror. She knew that bluff, frank voice; it always meant her father was at his most devious. She had better get downstairs before Fred invited Gil in for drinks and tried to pump him for information about the running of Westbrooks. Gil would not appreciate that.

She ran downstairs, hearing their voices in the hall, and Gil turned to watch her come, his dark eyes narrowed in an appraisal which made her acutely self-conscious.

Her father stared, too, bolt-eyed and frowning. 'Wherever did you buy that?' he growled disapprovingly. She had expected his reaction; her father usually was conservative when it came to her clothes, and the neckline of the flame-coloured dress was much lower than her necklines usually were, revealing the pale curve where her breasts began. The clinging silky skirt was tight-fitting, but slit up one side, giving a glimpse of her thigh with every step she took. Caro had hesitated over buying the dress for ages; she had never been prepared to take risks where clothes were concerned, but tonight she had been feeling rebellious and her mirror told her the flame dress really did something for her.

'She bought it at Westbrooks,' drawled Gil, and she gave him a startled look. He intercepted it and grinned at her. 'Oh, yes, I recognise our stock! I don't just sit behind my desk and dictate memos, you know! I can even tell you how much it cost and which firm made it.'

'Good lad,' Fred approved, beaming. 'I like a man who keeps in touch with what he's selling, even when his store is as big as Westbrooks.'

Gil gave him a sardonic glance. 'But you'll still take my job away and hand the running of my store over to one of your own executives.'

'We haven't even begun to think about it!' Fred stoutly said, and Caro knew from the faint shift of his eyes that he was lying.

Gil was right, she realised. Her father had already decided to replace him with one of their own men. Her stomach turned over sickeningly and she paled. Gil was going to hate her when it happened. He would never forgive either her or her father.

CHAPTER SEVEN

THE party was held in one of the leafy streets of St John's Wood, close to Caro's own district of London, and a very chic, elegant and expensive place to live. It had once been the fashionable place for married Victorian gentlemen to keep their expensive mistresses, which was why the houses were often imitations of overgrown country cottages set among pretty cottage gardens, with pink tiled roofs and little porches, and stained glass windows to give a spuriously pious air. The district had changed a great deal, of course. Today there were plenty of blocks of flats and ugly modern buildings, and the streets were choked by traffic, but the trees and gardens persisted and somehow that country feeling still clung on.

The party was in full swing by the time they arrived. Amy met them at the door, flushed with excitement and as graciously welcoming as if she was giving the party herself. She kissed Caro on her cheek, lightly, then stood back and eyed her up and down, lifting her eyebrows in laughing disbelief. 'Well, well, well! Darling, what's happened to you?'

Caro felt waves of heat flow up her face, especially with Gil smilingly observing her, but fortunately Amy didn't wait for a reply. She had already turned and kissed Gil, not quite so lightly, or so quickly. Her mouth lingered, and she smiled up into his eyes, tiny, childlike, oddly sexy Amy.

'Hello, again,' she cooed in her throatiest voice. 'I was afraid you wouldn't actually come. I'm so glad you have—it will give us a chance to get to know each other better.'

'I hope so,' Gil said softly, staring into her baby-blue eyes with unhidden amusement.

Caro watched, not sure whether she was more jealous or envious. Her teeth were tight and her throat smouldered with fury over the way Amy was flirting with him, but she knew, too, that she wished she could frankly react to a man the way Amy did. She was too shy, though, too self-conscious. Amy wasn't; she was never inhibited or nervous. She had a most enviable gift of self-assurance and enjoyment of life.

'You must come and say hello to some people who are dying to meet you,' Amy said to him, threading her arm through his. Casually, she tossed to Caro the remark that, 'Antony is over there, at the bar, handing out the drinks. He's been waiting for you with bated breath since the party began. Go and help him, there's a love!'

Caro glanced across the room to where a very tall, very skinny man with a rugged, raw-boned face and pale, fine hair was pouring drinks and offering bowls of peanuts. He wasn't at all bad-looking, she decided, but then even if she had hated him she wouldn't have admitted it in front of Gil. She forced a bright smile and said, 'Love to! See you!'

She felt Gil watching her, but didn't look his way to check on his expression. What difference did it make? Amy was going to monopolise him all evening, and anyway, Gil loathed and despised both her and her father. She was just torturing herself by thinking about him. They were enemies and would never be anything else.

When Fred had blandly claimed that he hadn't even begun to think about possible future changes at Westbrooks, Gil had known he was lying. He hadn't bothered to argue. Her face had tightened and hardened, but he had just said quietly to her, 'If you're ready, we'll be on our way.'

She normally kissed her father before she went out in the evenings, but tonight she had just walked out, without even looking at Fred Ramsgate. No doubt that would have surprised and puzzled her father, but she hadn't cared.

Gil had put her into the front passenger seat of the black Rolls and had driven away without speaking to her, scowling through the windscreen at the light traffic through which they had moved. Caro had known what he was thinking about—what else could make him look like that? She had wished she could come up with something to distract him, but her mind had been numb with guilt and unhappiness. This was the first time that she had actually begun to realise the human consequences of one of their takeover operations. Hitherto she had told herself that they would improve a department store; make money for everybody, including the staff and the shareholders. But then in the past she had never been emotionally involved with any of the management they were ousting.

She put a bright smile on her face as she went up to Antony. 'Hi! I'm a friend of Amy...'

'I remember,' he said vaguely, pouring her a drink and handing it to her with an automatic smile. 'You're Caro. We met when I operated on Amy, and she's always talking about you; schoolgirl chums, weren't you?' He let his pale blue eyes roam over the flame-red dress and his smile brightened. 'You look gorgeous, I love the dress. Have you come to help me behind the bar? Won't you come into my parlour, said the spider to the fly...?' He waved her round to his side of the polished wood counter. 'Tell you what, you deal with those who want wine and I'll deal with the rest, OK?'

'OK,' she said bleakly, her eyes on the other side of the room where Amy was twining herself all over Gil, like clinging ivy around a tall tree.

Antony followed her stare and grimaced. 'Sometimes I could kill her,' he said with grim frankness.

Caro looked at at him. 'You're in love with her?'

'How did you guess?' he said drily.

'It wasn't difficult,' she said with sympathy, wondering if her own state of the heart was as obvious. She must stop looking at Gil; she had an uneasy suspicion that her feelings showed when she was looking at him.

'I made the mistake of caring more than she did,' Antony told her in a bright voice, pretending to find it all funny. 'Amy loves to be in love, but it wears off quickly and then she gets bored. I'm unfortunately the faithful type. Very silly of me, but there you are...I can't help it.'

Caro felt so sorry for him—and for herself. She could almost have cried. She leaned over and kissed him. 'I'm so sorry. Love's hell, isn't it?'

'You find it hell, too?' he guessed, and she wished she hadn't been so frank. She didn't want to talk about Gil, or about herself.

'I was in love once,' she said lightly. 'Years ago— Damian Shaw, his name was. He was a swine and I was broken-hearted, but it always passes, you know. You just have to let time be the doctor.'

He laughed. 'A better one than I am, I'm sure. So you're fancy free again? Nobody else has come along since the swine?'

She shook her head and to change the subject poured him a drink. 'Come on, cheer yourself up and enjoy the fun!'

He shook his head, smiling. 'I'd better not. I'm in charge of this party, and if I get drunk heaven only knows what will happen.'

There was a sudden rush of people wanting drinks and for ten minutes they hardly exchanged a word. When they did start talking again, Caro took care to keep the conversation light. She asked about his work, about the new flat, about his family, about his hobbies—anything, in fact, except what was on both their minds. Amy and Gil were dancing now, very close together because the room was small and there were too many others dancing in it. They all shuffled around, arms around each other, bodies touching. Caro wouldn't look. Couldn't bear to look. But she knew exactly how they danced, how they gazed at each other, how they smiled. And she hated it.

'Like to dance?' somebody asked and Caro looked round, startled. The young man was a complete stranger, but Antony knew him and pushed her towards him, smiling.

'Caro, meet Peter. He's the world's worst physician, but he can dance, so go on, enjoy yourself!'

'Well, thank you.' The young man grinned, sliding an arm round Caro before she could think of an excuse not to dance. They moved into the throng and shuffled with everybody else. Caro was very flushed and overheated and wished she could go home; she wished she hadn't come, in fact. She wished she could see Gil, but although she spotted Amy nearby, she was dancing with somebody else and there was no sign of Gil. Had he gone home? Caro's stomach plunged and she felt miserable, until she caught sight of him at the bar, getting a drink.

A moment later Amy announced that food was being served in the kitchen and everyone began pushing that way. Caro excused herself to her partner and went back to the bar. Gil was still leaning on it, sipping a large glass of iced lime and soda.

'Isn't it hot in here?' Caro said, thirstily staring at his drink. 'I could do with one of those.'

He offered her his glass. 'Oh, I couldn't take yours!' she said, but he insisted, so she sipped from it gratefully.

'Thank you, that was delicious...' she said, giving it back to him. 'My throat was parched.'

'Do you want some supper?' he asked, finishing the drink and putting down the glass. 'Amy showed it to me, and I must say it looks fabulous. She has quite a gift for organisation, doesn't she? A very shrewd girl, too.'

Caro wondered what he meant by that. It was true, Amy was shrewd, but in what way had Gil meant it? She wasn't going to ask, of course. Instead, she said, 'Please, do go and get some food, if you want to eat...'

He shook his head. 'I'm not hungry, but I'll get you a plateful...'

'No, I'm not hungry, either,' she said.

There was a silence, then Gil asked quietly, 'Do you want to stay here? Are you enjoying it?'

She took a deep breath and told the truth. It was quite a relief. 'Not really; I don't know many people and it's rather overcrowded and much too hot. What about you?' She looked up into his dark eyes and Gil smiled wryly.

'I'm bored out of my skull. Let's get out of here, and we'd better not find Amy to tell her we're going. Hang on…' He went over to where Antony was lining up clean glasses, freshly brought from the dishwasher in the kitchen. Gil told him they were going and Antony waved to her, grinned broadly.

'Have fun, you two!'

Caro flushed and that made Antony laugh aloud. As they left, she asked Gil crossly, 'What did you say to him?'

'I said we were going off to a private party of our own!' Gil drawled, putting her into the front seat of the Rolls. Caro's face was burning. She had a feeling her ears were, too.

'Oh, how could you?' she muttered, sinking down into the deeply upholstered leather seat. 'He'll probably repeat that to Amy and then she'll spread it around half London!'

'Who are you afraid will hear about it?' Gil got into the seat beside her and started the engine. 'Damian Shaw?'

She did a double-take. 'What?'

'I heard all about it from Amy,' said Gil and Caro's teeth met.

'Amy had no right to talk about my private life!' she muttered. Why had Amy talked about Damian to him? How dared Amy discuss something so intimate about a friend with a man she had only just met? But Caro knew why, of course; her grey eyes glittered. She had always known that Amy could be ruthless, but she hadn't thought Amy would ever betray her! But then they had never been in possible competition for the same man before! She saw with bitter clarity that Amy had sensed her interest in Gil; Amy had known her a long time and knew her very well. If Amy had told Gil about Damian it was so that Gil would think she was in love with someone else and wouldn't take any interest in her himself.

'But everyone seems to know about him,' Gil retorted as they purred through St John's Wood. 'He's hardly a deeply buried secret. First Amy, then the guy you were helping at the bar—was he the one giving the party? Well, he mentioned Damian Shaw to me, too.' He gave her a sideways glance, his mouth twisting. 'They both seemed to think you were still in love with him. Still carrying a torch for him, as Amy put it—are you?'

'That's my business!' she muttered, staring past the amber street lights to the darker pools of shadow where the park lay. They were almost home, she would soon get away from him and be alone to cope with this tearing pain inside her breast.

'Partly mine, actually,' Gil coolly said. 'Didn't you know he's one of my lawyers? He's taking part in the discussions with your father—surely he told you?'

Caro's head swung; she stared at him, grey eyes wide, mouth parted in shock and disbelief.

'Apparently not,' Gil thought aloud, staring back at her, and another car shot past them, blaring angrily as Gil's car drifted across the road while his attention was on Caro. Gil swore and turned his eyes back on the road ahead. 'I wonder why your father didn't say anything?'

Caro knew why. Her father was well aware of that old affair and why it had ended. He had played a considerable part in ending it. He had suspected Damian from the start, and when there had been talk of an engagement he had put a private detective on his tail to check up on him, and had discovered the other woman in Damian's life.

Damian had been having an affair with one of his typists for months. They had met in hotel bedrooms on evenings when he told Caro he was working late; they had gone away together for the weekend and he'd told Caro he had to visit a client abroad and couldn't take her. Caro hadn't at first believed a word of the report her father had grimly showed her. She had pushed it away, shaking her head, white and trembling, but there had been too much irrefutable evidence. Photographs, testimony by hotel staff, photocopies of hotel registers. They had always signed in as a married couple, under a false name, of course. Caro still remembered the way she had felt staring at the girl's face—she'd been nineteen, blonde, very pretty. One look and Caro had known Damian was a liar and a cheat. He had planned to marry her for her money, but he had had no intention of being faithful to her. That was so humiliating that for months afterwards she had wanted to die. It was bad enough that he hadn't ever loved her, that he had wanted to marry her only for her father's money, but it was far more wounding to know that even if he had married her he would have betrayed her with other women all the time; their marriage would have been a complete lie.

'Doesn't your father approve of Shaw?' asked Gil. 'I suppose he wanted you to marry someone with more money. Did he interfere? Order you to stop seeing him? Is that what happened?'

'No, it isn't!' she snapped, her loyalty to her father forcing her to answer. 'You don't know my father. He isn't some old-fashioned domestic tyrant. He doesn't judge people by how much money they have, and he has never once ordered me to stop seeing anyone.'

'Amy seemed to think otherwise,' said Gil drily.

'How much did she tell you, for heaven's sake?' Caro muttered, dark red and furious.

'Something about a private detective...'

'I'll kill her, I'll really kill her!' She hesitated, breathing thickly, then reluctantly said, 'OK, Dad did pay a private detective to follow Damian, but only because he had suspicions about him and wanted to check him out, and he was proved right. He found out that... Well, anyway, it was all true. I didn't just take Dad's word for it. I faced Damian with the photos and other evidence, and Damian didn't deny any of it. He couldn't.'

Gil slowed and pulled up under a tree whose drooping branches hung low over the road. 'Another woman?' he asked curtly, and she nodded without looking at him.

'Oh, he tried to tell me that it hadn't meant anything,' she said with cynicism in her voice. 'He claimed that he'd been "seduced" by this other girl, he put all the blame on her. If you'd seen her picture!' Her mouth writhed and her eyes glittered angrily. 'She was a pretty kid of about nineteen, younger than me! She was probably as innocent as a newborn lamb until she met him. But Damian painted her as some sort of *femme fatale*—it was all her fault. He said he'd loved me all the time, the other thing had been a passing madness, and he would end the affair at once, if I would forgive him.'

'But you didn't,' said Gil, his eyes intent on her angry face.

'I did not. Would you have done?'

He shook his head, mouth twisting. 'It sounds to me as if you were well out of that relationship!'

Having started to talk about it, Caro couldn't seem to stop. She said bitterly, 'I listened to him lying and wriggling and blaming the other girl, and I started to hate him. He's a very convincing lawyer, because he's as cunning as a wagonload of monkeys, and I'm sure he does a great job for you, but I wouldn't trust him further than I could throw him.'

'He still seems to arouse a powerful reaction in you, though,' Gil drawled, watching her closely. 'They say hatred is the flip side of love. Are you sure you're over him?'

She laughed harshly. 'Absolutely certain! And I don't even hate him now, I just despise him.'

'Well, let's just see, shall we?' His voice had an odd intonation and she was so puzzled by that that she looked up at him just as he bent towards her, which made it easier for him. His mouth was on hers before she had any idea what he meant to do; the feel of it was hard and warm, deeply intimate, possessive; and a tidal wave of emotion hit her, her lips parted under his, and her head swam. She felt everything cloud inside her mind, she was dizzy and blind with passion, and her hands instinctively reached for his shoulders, clinging to him in case she actually fell.

When Gil finally lifted his head again, she looked dazedly at him, feeling a deep sense of loss, aching for him to kiss her again. Gil studied her through half-closed lids, his dark eyes gleaming like hidden water. What was he thinking about? She knew so little about him, how his mind worked; he was a mystery to her, even though she had been seeing him every day, lately, for hours at a time.

When he did speak she was puzzled by the question. 'How old were you when you met Shaw?' he asked in that deep, velvety voice of his, and she was so surprised that she automatically answered.

'Twenty-one.' It seemed a lifetime ago; how young and stupid she had been! She felt quite sorry for her half-forgotten self.

'And how many men have there been since?' She hesitated, looking away, breathless, and Gil gave a short laugh. 'From the way you react to me whenever I touch you, I'd guess there have been very few—if there have been any! Shaw left you in a deep-freeze and you've been existing in it ever since, haven't you? I remember how you flew into a temper when I suggested that you'd never been to bed with anyone. Did you sleep with Shaw?' He stared fixedly at her, watching the involuntary flicker of her lids, the deepening heat in her face. 'No, I don't think you had got that far. You were very young and he planned to marry you, not just seduce you. You were business; he had the other girl for his playtime.'

Caro flinched at the bluntness of that. It was the truth, of course, but her ego still stung at the reminder. Gil noted her expression, his dark eyes narrowed.

'That bothers you?' he said coldly. 'If you're still jealous over him, it means you haven't stopped caring about the man.'

'I am not jealous! And I certainly don't care anything about him, I just told you ... I despise him.'

'So it won't bother you to see him again?'

'What?' She stiffened, her face tight and cold, staring back at him, and Gil watched her with that probing fixity as he said,

'Well, it is on the cards, isn't it?'

'What are you talking about?'

'For a woman with a first-rate brain, you can be very stupid!' Gil snapped. 'Think about it! You've been too busy working on the accounts at Westbrooks to sit in on any of the meetings your father has been having with my grandmother's people, but sooner or later you're likely to be called in to discuss the report you've submitted, and then you're going to come face to face with Damian Shaw. How are you going to feel then?'

'I won't feel anything,' she lied, and Gil laughed shortly.

'Oh, come off it! It's obvious he's still under your skin!'

That made her even angrier, and she burst out, 'Under my skin? You must be joking! Can't you see how humiliating it was...finding out how I'd been cheated? He made me believe he loved me, but he was laughing at me behind my back. He pretended to think I was pretty, and I let him fool me into believing it, even though my mirror told me I was crazy—and all the time he was sneaking off to see another girl, and she really was pretty! He didn't have to lie to her. She wasn't a rich man's daughter; he was genuinely attracted to her. With me he was just lying. I felt sick when I knew—I can never forget the humiliation, but that isn't because I still care about Damian, it's because he made me face the fact that the only reason a man was showing interest in me was because of my father's money.'

She stopped speaking, taking an appalled breath, suddenly realising what she was saying, who she was saying it to! She had told Gil Martell what she had never told another living soul, what she had thought she would never be able to confide to anyone—the depth and bitterness of her humiliation over her betrayal by Damian. She looked down, face first crimson then white, biting her lip and wishing she was dead. Why on earth had she let all that spill out of her? And to him, of all people, the last man in the world she wanted to know how much of a fool she had been!

Tears began trickling down her cheek; she had to choke back a sob trying to force its way out of her.

'Don't,' Gil said harshly, and then both his arms went round her, pulling her closer; he put a hand on the back of her head, pushing it down on to his chest, and began gently to stroke her hair. She lay against him, trembling, her eyes closed, beginning to calm as the comforting caress of his fingers continued.

His human warmth soaked into her, permeating her entire body until she was able to relax completely in his arms, giving herself up to a deep contentment. It was a sensation she had never felt with Damian; she had been feverish and unsure whenever she was with him, so perhaps her instincts had warned her, even though she hadn't listened to them. Her instincts now told her to trust Gil, whispered that she was safe with him...

She started as a strange bleeping noise began somewhere close by—what on earth was that? She thought for a second she was imagining it, hearing things, but then Gil gave an exasperated sigh, his arms dropping away from her. He sat up, and Caro lay back against her seat, reluctantly opening her eyes to watch Gil reach down to produce a phone from between the front seats of the Rolls. Only as the noise stopped did Caro realise that it was the sound of a car phone.

'Yes?' Gil barked into his receiver, and then his face changed as he listened. 'Oh, hello, Mrs Greybury. Is something wrong?' There was a brief silence, then he exclaimed, 'What?' His brows dragged together, he listened again, his face tightened. 'Oh, did she? Look, tell her I won't be back until tomorrow...Oh, you did?' His long, slim fingers tapped out an angry rhythm on the wheel as he listened again. 'Did she? Won't leave until I get back. I see.' He stared straight ahead, scowling, a dark red in his cheeks, his eyes glittering with temper. 'Right,' he said. 'I'll be back in a few minutes, then.'

He replaced the phone with a slam that made Caro jump. 'I'm sorry,' he said curtly to her. 'I have to get back to my flat at once.'

'An unexpected visitor?' Caro swallowed a jealousy which tasted like poison.

'You were listening?'

She didn't like the ice in his voice and snapped back, 'I could hardly help overhearing you! I didn't exactly eavesdrop outside the door.'

'OK, OK,' he muttered. 'I'm sorry, I didn't mean to snarl. My temper snapped.'

'I noticed,' she said coldly.

He laughed as the car began to move away. 'Your tongue will get you into trouble one of these days!'

She watched his long hands manipulate the wheel, feeling weak with desire. Why did he make her feel this way? She had never wanted anything so much in her life before. Oh, why did he have to be involved with another woman? Was every man she ever met going to prefer someone else? Was that her doom? Life was very unfair.

'It's the Countess, isn't it?' she asked, then wanted to kick herself for such a stupid question. Who else could it be? Trying to hide how much it hurt her, she spoke lightly, mockingly. 'Has she left her husband again? It's getting to be a habit; why doesn't she make up her mind?'

'She has, it seems,' Gil said. 'My housekeeper says Miranda has moved in, with a mound of luggage. In fact, she has started to unpack.'

Caro felt sick. 'Congratulations!' she managed, forcing an over-bright smile.

'Don't be funny,' Gil muttered. 'And stop talking to me. I'm trying desperately to think of a way to get rid of her before Colin arrives, but Miranda isn't easy to talk round. She only sees things from her own point of view. Totally spoilt and totally selfish, and a brain the size of a flea into the bargain—you can't talk sense to a woman like that. She only understands flattery or flirtation, and I'm in no mood to try either.'

Caro sat upright, tense and still, and watched his hard profile intently. He wasn't talking like a man in love; his voice was impatient, irritated, his face matched his tone. Was this what he really felt, or was he pretending?

'You must have given her the idea that you would want her...' she began, and Gil groaned, raking a hand through his dark hair.

'Oh, maybe, a few compliments, a little game of flirtation at a party; women like Miranda expect it, but there was never anything between us, nothing serious, nothing that meant anything——' He broke off, frowning darkly. 'Except that...'

'That she took it seriously, even if you didn't?' guessed Caro, her mouth twisting.

'Women always do,' he said with weary cynicism. 'Their vanity makes them think you're crazy over them. They want it to be the real thing, every time. Love with a capital L. They like it to be forever, not just fun.'

Caro felt a flare of rage so intense she wanted to hit him. 'You deserve to be landed with the Countess! You talk about her being spoilt and selfish! You could give her lessons.'

He ignored that, pulling up outside his flat, peering out of the car window. 'No sign of Colin's car yet, anyway. That gives me time to get Miranda out of there— if only I can think of the way to convince her she must go...'

'I ought to walk away and leave you to it,' Caro thought aloud, hating him. 'I shouldn't help you get out of it.'

Gil turned a hopeful look on her, his dark eyes pleading. 'Have you got an idea how I could get rid of her? Tell me.'

'I don't think I should.' Caro considered him scornfully. 'You've asked for this. How many other women have you flirted with and then dumped?'

'I'm not some sort of monster,' he claimed, looking at her coaxingly, all innocence. 'Come on, Caro—you don't want Miranda to gobble me up, do you?'

'Yes,' she said, almost meaning it. It had made her deeply angry to hear him talk about women's vanity, mocking a woman's need to find love, to know the real thing at last and believe it was forever. A few minutes ago, she had been in his arms, her stupid heart beating like mad because she believed she loved him and that this time it was real, this time it was forever. If Gil ever guessed he would make cynical jokes about her, too; laugh at her, mock her. He must never know how she felt.

She looked at him with dislike. 'But then even Miranda doesn't deserve you! For her sake, I suppose I'll have to come to the rescue.'

She didn't wait for him to respond to that. She opened the car door and got out. Gil slid out of the driver's seat, too, but Caro turned and shook her head at him. 'No, you stay here. I'll deal with this alone.'

He stood on the other side of the car, staring at her, his hair blown by the night breeze, his face uncertain. 'What are you going to say to her? If you're thinking of appealing to her finer feelings, don't. She hasn't got any. Miranda's only feelings are reserved for Miranda, and in this case she is using me to punish her husband and she doesn't care whether Colin breaks every bone in my body, or whether I beat Colin to a pulp, so long as she can be there to watch it happen.'

'If I'm to help you, I must have a free hand to tell her what I like,' Caro said remotely, looking away from the sight of that lean, powerful body of his and reminding herself that the mind inside it was by no means as attractive. 'Is that agreed?'

'OK,' he said after a little silence. 'Tell her what you like, I'll leave it all to you—but for heaven's sake get rid of her as soon as possible, before Colin comes galloping up and tries to kill me.'

'I would hold his horse while he did it,' Caro promised him, turning to walk towards the front door.

'Aren't you going to tell me what you're going to say?' Gil asked, and she nodded.

Over her shoulder she told him, 'I shall say we're getting married next week.'

CHAPTER EIGHT

GIL sat staring after her in utter silence, and Caro had the satisfaction of knowing that for once she had caught him off guard; in fact, she had taken his breath away.

Eyes gleaming with amusement, she put out a hand to ring the bell, but at that instant the door opened. Caro guessed at once that this must be Gil's housekeeper, a small, neat woman in a dark dress, with carefully styled grey hair, who stared at her in an obvious surprise which rapidly became weary disapproval. Caro read that expression without difficulty. Mrs Greybury believed her to be yet another young woman pursuing Gil. How many had there been in the past, for heaven's sake? thought Caro, tightening her mouth. It was high time that man was taught a lesson.

'Mr Martell is not at home,' Mrs Greybury said, beginning to close the door.

Caro put a foot in the door to stop her and at the same time shot a glance over Mrs Greybury's shoulder to make sure Miranda wasn't lurking somewhere behind her, like a spider waiting for a fly. There was no sign of her, though.

Keeping her voice low, Caro said, 'Actually, Mr Martell is sitting in his car out there. He drove me here.' She stood aside so that Mrs Greybury could see the Rolls, and the housekeeper stared a little myopically out into the street, started, gave a weak smile, lifted a hand and waved before hurriedly snatching her hand down again, as if afraid she looked silly.

'Isn't he coming in?' she warily asked.

Caro shook her head. 'He feels safer out there.'

'I've no doubt he does,' the housekeeper grimly said, then studied Caro more closely. 'Are you coming in?' Caro nodded and Mrs Greybury asked then, 'Did he send you?' Caro nodded. Mrs Greybury considered her again, head on one side. 'To get something for him?' she hazarded.

Caro shook her head. 'To deal with the Countess for him.'

Mrs Greybury made a strange noise, something like a kettle getting ready to boil.

'Yes, men are helpless, aren't they?' Caro agreed sympathetically, interpreting the sound. 'Well, we'd better get on with it. Where is she?'

Mrs Greybury stepped aside, pointing along the wide, cream-painted hall. 'Third door on the left.'

'The spare bedroom?'

The housekeeper nodded, gave her a discreetly curious look. 'Er—may I ask...who...?'

'Who I am?' guessed Caro, smiling. 'I'm Caroline Ramsgate, Mrs Greybury. Mr Martell and I are engaged.'

Mrs Greybury's famed discretion deserted her briefly. Her mouth dropped open. 'Engaged?' she repeated incredulously.

Caro nodded, giving her an earnest stare. 'You will remember that, won't you? If anyone should ask. Like the Countess, for example? I am Mr Martell's fiancée. OK?'

Mrs Greybury's eyes narrowed. 'Ah,' she said.

Caro grinned. 'Exactly. Now, don't forget.'

'No,' the housekeeper promised, staring hard at Caro. She smiled back quite suddenly, as if she had just made up her mind what she thought of Caro. 'Oh, no, don't worry, I won't get it wrong.'

'Mr Martell said I could rely on you,' Caro lied, and the housekeeper's face lit up like a Christmas tree.

'Did he really say that?'

Touched by that delight, Caro nodded, then turned and headed down the hall towards the third door. She couldn't help noticing the casually elegant style of the furnishing, the polished wood-block floor, the gilt-framed mirror, the floor-length cream brocade curtains at the windows, the Georgian hall-table and the large Chinese vase into which were thrust umbrellas and walking sticks. Through the open door she passed she saw a spacious sitting-room furnished in much the same way, a very English décor, comfortably classy and in restful colours. She approved Gil's taste; it was something else about him she liked.

She tapped firmly on the third door, taking a deep breath when she heard the voice inside say sharply, 'Who is it?' It was a very familiar voice, and one she disliked intensely.

Caro tapped again without answering, and after a brief pause the door was pulled open and the Countess said crossly, 'Well, what do you want?' Her voice died away as she saw Caro. She stared, her eyes narrowing with hard suspicion.

Caro stared back, bitterly noticing yet again just how lovely she was, slender as a reed in her lace-trimmed ivory silk négligé, her blonde hair shimmering. She looked perfect for an instant; radiant as daybreak, innocent as a white rose. You had to look closely to see the ice glittering in those big blue eyes, the selfish line of that beautifully modelled mouth. Men probably never looked at her hard enough. They were too dazzled by their first quick glance and then in too much of a hurry to catch this butterfly which had fluttered through their lives to bother to look any closer.

The Countess was observing Caro in her turn, looking her up and down with a curling, dismissive smile. 'I've seen you before, haven't I?' she said. 'You were at Gil's grandmother's house the other evening, when I had dinner there. You're that girl, the Ramsgate girl. I gather your father's buying Westbrooks.'

'That's right,' Caro said pleasantly, moving forward with such determination that the Countess had to fall back into the room. Caro let her gaze roam around, noting the disorder. Suitcases flung open with their contents displayed, clothes draped everywhere, dresses on hangers in a mahogany wardrobe, piles of silky undies on the bed, or dropped haphazardly into a mahogany chest of drawers. Clearly the Countess planned to stay here for a long time.

A frown pleated the smooth forehead of the other woman. 'What exactly are you doing here, by the way?' she enquired with the casual arrogance of one accustomed to giving orders to servants. Caro met that blue gaze with a clear stare of her own.

'I'm waiting for my fiancé.'

Miranda looked blank. 'Your fiancé? Who's that?'

'Gil.' Caro's voice was soft and sweet, her grey eyes wide with innocent unawareness.

'What?' The shriek wasn't unexpected, yet it still made Caro jump. Miranda had turned first an ugly red and then gone white; not with pain, though, Caro sensed, watching her closely. No, Miranda was white with temper, her mouth was trembling with it and her blue eyes spat a rage that made Caro back slightly in alarm.

'I don't believe you! You're lying. You and Gil? Gil, marry you? Don't make me laugh, as if he would look twice at you!' Miranda ran scornful eyes over her from head to foot. 'You're not just plain, you're downright ugly, and you have the dress sense of a blind camel. Look at that red thing! Vulgar. Horribly, embarrassingly vulgar. Neckline down to your waist and as for that slit up the side...well, really! I've no doubt you put it on to catch Gil's eye, but you're wasting your time, he doesn't go for anything that obvious. Gil has too much taste.'

Caro kept very calm, although it was not easy. She went on smiling, even if it made her teeth ache, and she forced her voice to sound cheerful and polite, as though the Countess had not just insulted her grossly and was not at this moment looking at her with hatred and fury.

'We're getting married next week,' she told Miranda in a conversational tone. 'Family and really close friends only; it's going to be a very quiet wedding. We both hate the idea of a lot of fuss and publicity.'

'No!' Miranda yelled. 'It isn't true. He wouldn't——'

'The announcement will come afterwards, once we're on our honeymoon,' Caro added, as if she hadn't heard a word of what Miranda was saying.

Miranda grabbed her shoulders and shook her violently. 'Stop lying! It's all lies, all of it.'

As if on cue there was a tap on the door and Mrs Greybury appeared, calm and polite, smoothing down her dress with pale hands. 'May I help you pack again, my lady?' she enquired and Miranda glared at her.

'I'd forgotten you! You must know! Listen, is Mr Martell getting married?'

'Next week, my lady,' Mrs Greybury said, picking up the piles of delicate lacy underwear and beginning to pack them back into Miranda's cases.

'We'll be moving in here at first, and as I'm always so busy at work, Mrs Greybury will carry on just as she always has done—but then we thought later we might like a house nearer the park, near my father's house. We're very close, you know, and with Gil's grandmother living just a short walk away it will be perfect,' Caro said. She was enjoying this, in an angry way; enjoying making Miranda so furious, even though Miranda's long fingers and pointy red nails were quite painful, and it wasn't much fun being shaken like that. It made her feel slightly giddy.

'I've packed these two cases; I'll take them into the hall and ring for a taxi for you, my lady,' Mrs Greybury said, departing with a case in each hand.

'I'm not going anywhere!' Miranda yelled after her and gave Caro another shake to emphasise the point.

'Do stop doing that,' Caro complained softly. 'I might be sick, and you wouldn't want that, would you?'

Miranda's eyes rounded; she gave a gasp. 'I see it all now! Oh, you scheming little... I know how you managed it. You've got yourself pregnant!'

Caro couldn't help laughing. 'Now that would be one for the textbooks!'

Miranda, however, had no sense of humour and didn't even smile. 'You know what I mean! If Gil is going to marry you, there has to be a reason—I know he can't be in love with you.' That stung, but Caro refused to let it show. She went on smiling. 'Either you're expecting his baby—or have told him you are!—because I simply don't believe he would ever bring himself to marry you.' Caro went on smiling. Damn you, damn you, she thought, tears burning somewhere behind her bright, shiny eyes.

'Or else...' the Countess slowly said, staring at her. 'Or else he's marrying you to keep his store. That's it, isn't it? Your father means to buy Westbrooks and he will probably replace the top management—your sort of people always do, don't you? You buy a company and strip the assets and cut down on staff. So Gil will lose his store if your father buys it. But you're your father's only heir. You get all those department stores one day. My God, yes. I see it all now.'

'Think what you like,' Caro said, somehow managing to hang on to her temper. 'Just get out of here, will you?'

'Not until I've seen Gil!'

'Gil does not want to see you.'

'We'll see about that when he gets home.'

'He is home,' Caro said. 'He is sitting outside, waiting for you to leave.'

Miranda looked at her, ran to the window and pulled aside the curtain to stare out into the street. Caro felt sorry for her for an instant, seeing her body as tense as a violin bow. Was she genuinely in love with Gil? Was she unhappy? Then Caro hardened her heart against the other woman. Miranda had a husband and a life elsewhere; let her go to them and leave Gil alone. Gil had asked Caro to help him, and she was going to do just that, whatever the cost to herself.

Miranda suddenly ran towards the door, screaming, 'Gil! Gil!' Caro followed her, realising that she could hardly stop her speaking to him. They passed Mrs Greybury in the hall.

'The taxi is on its way, my lady,' she blandly said. 'I'll finish packing for you, shall I?'

Miranda didn't answer; she had pulled the front door open and was running to Gil. Caro stood in the doorway and watched him open the limousine door and swing his long legs out of the Rolls. He straightened, then leaned casually against it, a very tall, elegant man, with dark, wind-ruffled hair, his expression unreadable at this distance. How did he really feel about Miranda? She wished she knew. Caro knew how she, herself, felt about Gil—her stomach plunged terrifyingly at the very sight of him. She couldn't blame Miranda for wanting him. She wanted him pretty badly herself.

She let Miranda get there and start sobbing all over him, then sauntered over to join them. 'The Countess's taxi will be here soon, Gil, darling,' she said, her grey eyes meeting his dark ones over Miranda's bent head. 'I told her our wonderful news, by the way. What a pity we can't have everyone to the wedding, but Dad insists on just family and really close old friends. We'll miss Miranda and her husband, won't we?'

'Oh, Gil, how could you?' Miranda accused. 'You're just marrying her to keep the store, aren't you?'

'Miranda, really!' Gil said reprovingly. 'Is that nice? Now, go and get dressed, there's a good girl.'

'I'm staying!' threatened Miranda. 'Send her away, darling. I must talk to you.'

'Oh, I'm spending the night here,' Caro coolly informed her.

Miranda made a violent gesture, gave a high-pitched whimper and then fled back indoors, her négligé flapping around her slender legs, her blonde hair dishevelled.

Gil breathed a long, deep sigh of relief. 'Let's hope she's really going.' He watched Caro's averted face. 'You constantly amaze me. I can never guess what you'll get up to next.'

She found it hard to keep cool now, in his presence; there was something about the way he was watching her that made her nerves prickle. 'You asked for help in getting rid of her, and this worked.' She tried to sound amused, and certainly he laughed.

'A week doesn't give us much time to think of an alternative, though,' he softly pointed out. 'If we don't get married next week, Miranda will be back.'

'You can always move,' Caro said. 'Or tell her frankly that you just aren't interested.' She lifted her grey eyes and met his stare. 'If you really aren't, that is!'

'I have never wanted to marry Miranda,' Gil said shortly. 'She can be fun, she can be very silly, she's obviously very beautiful. But Colin is an old friend; so is she, in fact. We've all known each other for years; I pushed her on her swing when she was a tot. I had a few dates with her before she decided she wanted to marry Colin. I think she loved him in the beginning. And she wanted his title, of course. It gave him a lot of glamour; all the girls swarmed round him. He hadn't started drinking then. He was very athletic, very fit; rode and swam and played rugger. Oh, yes, I think Miranda was in love with him once. I was best man at their wedding, and she was radiant. The trouble only started much later, when Colin's glamour wore off and he started to drink.'

'Sure that's the right way round? I mean, why did he start to drink? Could it be because he realised his wife preferred another man?' Miranda hadn't made any secret of it, either, Caro thought cynically.

Gil frowned. 'No, that only started quite recently. Colin has been drinking for quite a while, and I know Miranda tried hard to get him to stop. He called it nagging him, but she hated it when he came home drunk night after night.'

They both heard movements and fell silent just before Miranda reappeared, fully dressed again, her hair and face immaculate, her head up and her expression icily remote. Caro sighed, hoping they were not in for yet another scene, but at that instant a vehicle turned the corner and came towards them.

Gil looked round, raking his wind-blown hair back. 'Ah, here's your taxi, just on time. And here's Mrs Greybury with the rest of your suitcases. How many did you bring, darling? What amazing quantities of clothes you must wear every day.'

Miranda ignored him, flicking her eyes over the luggage to check that it was all there. The taxi pulled up beside her and the driver regarded the pile of cases with dismay. 'All that? How many passengers?'

'Just one,' Gil said. 'Here she is, waiting for you. I'll give you a hand loading her luggage.' He put several cases into the back of the cab while the driver put the rest in the front. Gil turned and bowed to Miranda courteously, offering his hand to help her into the taxi. 'Goodbye, Miranda, darling. We'll see you after the honeymoon.'

Miranda pretended not to see his outstretched hand; she climbed into the cab and sank back, crossing her long, slim legs elegantly.

'Where to?' asked the driver and Gil shrugged, closing the door on Miranda.

'Ask the lady.'

'Jurby House, Park Lane,' Miranda coldly said, and the taxi pulled away.

'She's going back to her husband,' Caro thought aloud, incredulously. 'I hope he throws her out again.

What consummate gall. And I wouldn't mind betting that she'll complain to him about you, too.'

'I'm sure you're right,' agreed Gil. 'I told you, Miranda is spoilt and self-obsessed, she only ever sees things from her own point of view.'

'What did you ever see in her?' Caro asked him, her mouth twisting, and he gave her a wry, amused smile.

'She's beautiful. One can't have everything.'

'So you did have an affair with her?' Caro immediately bit back, her grey eyes fierce, and Gil observed her mockingly.

'Every time you talk about her, you sound like a jealous woman.'

She was appalled because it was true; she was jealous, bitterly, sickeningly jealous. First scarlet, then white to her hairline, she turned blindly to walk towards the Rolls. 'Will you take me home, please?'

'Not yet,' he said coolly. 'Colin may arrive any minute and for the sake of our concocted alibi I think you had better be here with me, don't you?'

She opened her mouth to protest, but he took her elbow and firmly led her back into the flat. Mrs Greybury was hovering in the hall. 'Can I get you both a nightcap, sir?'

'Thank you, but I think we both need a brandy, and I'll get them. You get off to bed, Mrs Greybury. Goodnight, and thank you for all your help.'

'Goodnight, sir. Goodnight, Miss Ramsgate.'

'Oh...goodnight,' Caro said, turning to give the other woman a shy smile. Mrs Greybury smiled back and then vanished into another part of the flat.

Gill wandered into the sitting-room Caro had glimpsed earlier. She reluctantly followed and stood looking around her at the cool green and white of the décor:

tendrils of ivy on the wallpaper, floor-length green and white glazed chintz curtains, a green carpet and a white leather couch.

Gil poured them both a drink and turned to watch her slowly walk around the walls, looking at the paintings hanging there. She felt the back of her neck prickle, knowing he was watching her. Being alone with him was nerve-racking.

'Come and sit down,' he said in that deep dark voice, and she felt her heartbeat race out of all control.

'I'm admiring your taste in art,' she evaded, turning away to stare, without really seeing it, at a large, modern landscape hanging over the fireplace.

Gil came up behind her and she stiffened. He put a brandy glass into her hand. 'Drink this. It's been a rough evening.'

She hesitated, then obeyed, gasping at the heat of the spirits as they hit the back of her throat. The fumes seemed to mount to her brain, making her head swim. Gil swallowed his own brandy, put the empty glass down, took her glass away and put it down next to his own. Caro seemed rooted to the spot, standing on the hearth, her eyes fixed unseeingly on the painting.

Gil still stood behind her; she heard him breathing and her pulses went crazy. She wished he would go away, she wished he would...oh, do something! Not just stand there right next to her, almost touching her, tantalising her and driving her out of her mind.

At last she felt him move and held her breath, but he didn't walk away. He put a long finger on the nape of her neck and she shuddered with tension. The finger moved. Slowly. Down over her neck. Down her back. Very slowly. Caro closed her eyes, trembling. Gil moved closer, his body now touching hers. His lips lightly brushed her nape and she couldn't stop the audible intake of her breath, the gasp of shock and pleasure. He was killing her by inches, and she could not move, she was helpless to resist or fight the way she felt. I shouldn't have drunk that brandy, she thought. But even if she hadn't, would she have stopped him? The long finger stroked upwards from her waist; it stopped at the neckline of her dress and then she heard the zip unpeeling. That was when she should have stopped him, but she didn't because Gil's mouth followed the opening zip downwards, brushing light kisses along the widening gap and she was shaking, eyes enormous, pupils dilated with desire.

Gil's hands closed on her arms, his mouth burnt on her bare skin for a moment, while she trembled in his grip; then abruptly he whirled her round to face him and his head came down, his mouth seeking urgently.

Caro couldn't even think. She stood on tiptoe to meet his mouth, her lips parting with a sigh of hungry pleasure, her arms going round his neck. Gil enclosed her with one arm, his hand pressing into her back to hold her closer, while his other hand caressed her neck, pushed her dress down to bare her shoulders. Vaguely she became aware of her dress slipping to the floor. It didn't seem to matter; all that mattered was her need for his kiss. She pressed closer to Gil, holding his head in both hands, her fingers clenched in his thick hair.

He lifted her off the ground, his arms around her, still kissing her, and moved backwards to sink down on to the white couch. Caro opened her eyes then, pulled her head back, breathless and trembling. Gil held her on his lap, looking down into her grey eyes. He shrugged out of his jacket, tugged at his tie, pulled it off and let it fall to the carpet. She watched him undo his shirt, his lean body a pale tan colour, a rough wedge of dark hair growing up the centre of his muscled chest. Her mouth was dry. He watched her watching him; they stared at each other in a thick silence.

Caro had never watched a man undress before; her ears thundered with the sound of her own blood, her heart was thudding violently inside her ribcage, she almost felt he must be able to see it beating, through her skin, and he was staring down as if he could, staring at her half-naked body, the intimate probe of his dark eyes a sensuous excitement. He pushed down the straps of her slip and bra, bent and kissed her warm, bare breast, his lips and tongue seducing her, sending shivers of response through her.

'Touch me,' he whispered, and shyly at first, uncertainly, she reached out a hand to stroke, to caress, her fingertips so sensitised by then that when they first touched his bare skin it was like being given an electric shock; her whole body shuddered. His body was so cool and firm; she explored it, staring at him, and Gil watched her, his eyes half closed, his breathing thick. She began to moan; she had lost control; the common sense on which she prided herself snapped, and her senses took her into a new dimension of sensual intensity; she flung herself against him, her lips open against his shoulder, his neck, his chest, wordlessly pleading, begging, the hoarse cries of sexual need.

'Do you know what you're doing?' Gil said huskily, and she buried her face in him, unable to say the truth aloud. She knew, oh, she knew, and she wanted him too badly to care about what might happen afterwards. He shifted and pushed her down into the deep, yielding leather of the couch, his body rose above her, she saw through almost closed eyes the golden gleam of his naked skin as he shed the last of his clothes. Caro wriggled out of her own, keeping her eyes shut but knowing he watched her.

'I won't hurt you,' he said, brushing the hair back from her hot face. 'It is the first time for you, isn't it? The first time has to be good, you never forget it. I'll make it wonderful, Caro; something you won't want to forget.' He kissed her mouth, her throat, his lips gentle. His hands touched her breasts, her belly, her hips, brushing fire along her flesh, inciting her to a wild clamour of desire.

She moved against him with mounting urgency, moaning his name. 'Gil, Gil. Yes. Oh, yes...'

His hands were at her thighs, sliding between them, parting them, and his body followed, his bare skin smooth against her own for a moment before that first, tearing invasion. She gave a cry of pain, stiffening, and Gil murmured reassurance, 'Lie still, don't fight it, relax...' but the next move he made hurt even more and the heat drained out of her.

'No, stop,' she begged, and Gil lay very still on her for a moment or two. When he didn't move it no longer hurt, and she relaxed again, enjoying the warmth and pleasure of his body on her. He kissed her gently, stroked her hair. She kissed him back whispering, 'Sorry, I'm sorry...'

'No need to be,' he said, kissing her throat. 'No need to be sorry at all. I'm your first and that's a great compliment, I like that very much.' He kissed her breasts softly, first one and then the other, his tongue teasing, his hand splayed on her, spreading down over her flat belly to where their bodies had become one, and Caro gave a little groan of shock and pleasure at the brush of his fingertips there.

He kissed her mouth and her arms closed on his body, she arched against him in a remorseless return of desire, and Gil began to move again, very slowly, very gently, the rhythm building up until she was moving with him, her cries wild, her head thrown back.

Afterwards she felt as if she had fallen into a deep dark lake and drowned in abandonment. She lay in exhausted contentment, her body limp, and Gil lay beside her, his arm thrown across her, his head pillowed on her breast, his legs warmly twined with hers.

There was nothing to say, nothing that needed saying; happier than she had ever been in her life before, Caro slowly drifted into sleep.

A loud ringing shocked her awake; her eyes flew open, for a second not sure where she was, then she felt Gil's nakedness next to her, his hand on her breast, his legs pinning hers, and she remembered everything, and was at once crimson and couldn't look at him.

Gil swore huskily, sitting up. He looked down at her, as if amazed to see her, and Caro could have died. She shut her eyes, like a child who believed that that would make her invisible.

'Who the hell can be ringing at this hour?' he said and got off the couch. Opening her eyes, Caro had a disturbing glimpse of his body as he stalked over to a table where a telephone was ringing. Her mind played instant replays of their lovemaking and she had to bite her lip to stop herself groaning. She had begged him to make love to her. She could hear herself moaning, pleading. She wished she were dead.

Gil snatched up the phone. 'Yes?' he snapped, and then his face changed. He looked across the room at Caro, who was frantically dressing now, her hands fumbling, her face hotly flushed, her eyes shamed.

'Yes, she's here,' Gil said slowly.

Caro froze, looking at him in horrified query. 'It's your father, Caro,' Gil said in a flat, calm voice, but he didn't give her the phone. She could hear the loud and angry tones of her father's voice on the line. Gil listened, his mouth hard, and when Fred paused Gil quickly cut in.

'Yes, I realise what the time is... The party went on quite late and... Oh, you had a call from Amy? Yes, well, we did leave some time ago, but we came back here to have a nightcap——'

Fred's voice shouted him down for a moment; Caro couldn't hear what he was saying, but she knew that roar—her father was in a temper and trying to bully Gil. It did not seem to worry Gil, however. He interrupted Fred after a moment, his own voice brusque.

'Caro isn't a child. She's a woman; an adult woman. Why don't you let her get on with her own life?'

Caro had managed to get back into her dress now. She looked at her watch, horrified to see that it was four in the morning. She hurried over to grab the phone out of Gil's hand. 'I'll be home in ten minutes, Dad,' she said huskily and hung up before her father could say anything in reply.

'Could you get dressed quickly?' she asked Gil without actually looking at him. She didn't need to; she was deeply, disturbingly aware of his nakedness and the close proximity of that sexy body was sending heat waves through her.

He didn't move. 'Does he always wait up for you when you're out at night?' he said in a voice she did not like at all.

'No, but——' she began and he cut across her words.

'And does he always ring your date to complain if you aren't back by midnight? My God, I could understand it if you were a teenager, but you're apparently one of his top executives, a woman with a very important job. He seems to trust you at work—why doesn't he trust you to look after yourself on a date?'

'He usually does——'

'Oh? Then why check up on me?'

'I don't know,' she said irritably. 'He probably woke up and discovered I wasn't in, and was worried once he saw the time! I hadn't warned him I'd be out all night.'

'Do you have to have his permission?'

'No, of course not . . . but . . .'

'Do you often stay out all night?'

'No, I don't,' she said furiously, because she thought he was making too much of a natural anxiety on her father's part. 'That's probably why Dad was worried.'

'When is he going to let you grow up and take responsibility for yourself?' Gil drawled and moved towards her.

Caro leapt back, her whole body tense with panic. 'Don't touch me!'

Gil froze, and a silence settled over the room. Caro felt like crying. 'I'm sorry,' she said, miserably. 'But I can't stand any more. I'm too tired, it has been a long night. Could you get dressed?'

He walked away without another word, and, although she didn't look at him, she felt his physical presence with an intensity that frightened her. Her desire for him had not been sated by their lovemaking—it seemed to have been fed by it. She wanted him again—now.

'I'll take you home, when I'm dressed,' he said remotely, picking up his shirt and beginning to put it on.

'I can get a taxi home!' She swung towards the door, desperate to get away from him, but Gil snapped at her.

'I'll drive you. I brought you here, and I owe you a favour.' He paused, then added in a deep, sarcastic voice, 'Two favours.'

She winced at that, knowing all too well what he meant.

'And it is four in the morning, and I insist on seeing you safely home,' he said. 'Why don't you freshen up? The bathroom is two doors down.'

She was glad of an excuse to leave him alone to finish dressing. The bathroom was very masculine, elegantly functional, white, Victorian-style fittings in dark mahogany with blue and white wallpaper and curtains. Caro washed her hot face, patted it dry with one of the crisp white towels, looked with distaste at herself in the square, mahogany-framed mirror and tried to do something with her untidy hair. Her beautiful flame-red dress was crumpled, and there were faint red marks on her throat and shoulders, physical reminders of Gil's passion. She rearranged her dress to hide them, biting her lip. What if her father saw them?

She didn't go back to the room where Gil was dressing; she waited in the hall. When he came out he said curtly, 'I must go to the bathroom now; excuse me a moment, I won't keep you long.'

He spoke as if they were strangers, and she flinched, as if he had stabbed her. Gil vanished and she shut her eyes on a deep, painful sigh. He was angry with her; he probably regretted ever touching her. He had made love to her because he was unhappy over Miranda; it had been a crazy impulse, one he wished he hadn't given in to, and he blamed her.

Gil came back, his black hair freshly brushed, his face damp, but still unshaven so that his jaw showed a dark stubble. He paused to check that he had the keys to the Rolls, then opened the front door, gesturing to her to walk out first. It was half-past four now; dawn was breaking, a grey dawn which made London a city etched by half-light, the shapes of buildings looming out of the night here and there but the amber street lights still lit.

Gil pulled the front door shut behind them. Caro took her first breath of morning air, looking up at the sky to test the weather, and at that instant somebody darted towards them, apparently from nowhere. Caro gave a gasp, thinking at first that it was a mugger; they were being attacked.

Then there was a flash and she realised her mistake. Oh, they were under attack, all right, but not by thieves. This was a photographer, snatching shots of them. She gave a horrified wail and Gil leapt to her side, putting an arm round her, pushing her head into his chest and covering her face with his hand.

There was another flash, and then another, she heard Gil swearing and was aghast at the violence of the language. He let go of her to rush at the photographer who froze for a second, taking more rapid pictures, before running, with Gil in hot pursuit. Caro stood, shivering in the cold morning air, staring. A car engine started and a vehicle moved towards them; it slowed, a door flapping open at the passenger side, the photographer leapt in and then the car shot away. Gil chased it briefly but of course he had no chance of catching it. He came running back, face dark red, lungs panting, unlocked the Rolls and climbed behind the wheel.

'Get in!' he shouted at Caro, and she clambered in beside him. Before she could even slam the door, the

Rolls was moving. 'I want to follow the swine back to his lair,' Gil snarled. 'I bet he's the same fellow who snapped me fighting with Colin. Hasn't he got anything better to do than follow me around?'

Caro didn't need to answer that. They turned the corner but there was no longer any sign of the other vehicle. Gil swore again, and accelerated to the next street, but it was empty. They drove on for another few minutes before he admitted defeat; he had lost the other car.

He drew up, banging his long, powerful hands on the wheel, grinding his teeth in fury. 'Oh, if I ever get my hands on that guy. How does he always turn up at the wrong moment? Has he got second sight?' He scowled, his mouth a white line, stared at nothing for a moment, then turned slowly to stare at Caro. 'Somebody tipped him off,' he said, eyes narrowing. 'Somebody told him you were at my flat. Now why would somebody do that?'

Caro was puzzled. 'Do you think Miranda...?'

Gil went on staring fixedly at her. His face was hard and unsmiling; it frightened Caro, the way he was staring at her. What was he thinking?

'No, not Miranda,' he said. 'Her ego wouldn't want the rest of the world to know there was another woman in my flat.'

He was right, Caro saw that immediately. Miranda wouldn't spread this story, especially as she could only do so by explaining that she was at the flat herself and had been thrown out.

'Maybe the Press had been tipped off that Miranda was here?' she suggested.

'Then the photographer must have seen her leaving, and got his picture—why would he stay on after that?'

Caro shook her head, baffled. 'I don't know.' And why was he looking at her as if she were a caterpillar in his lettuce? Was she being blamed for this, too?

'Oh, of course you don't,' Gil said bitingly. 'Your father rings my flat to check you're with me and you insist on leaving right away, at four in the morning—and lo and behold! There's a photographer lurking outside.' He laughed shortly. 'Well, what an odd coincidence. But why didn't you have them waiting outside the window? What a picture they could have got earlier! That would have made a sensation!'

Caro got the point then. She turned scarlet, then paled. 'What on earth do I have to gain by getting myself photographed with you?' she asked him angrily.

'You tell me!' Gil said, and then he drove on very fast without another word. She sat beside him, burning with indignation. How could he suspect her of doing such a thing? What possible reason could she have?

He pulled up outside her home with a jolt of brakes and a screech of tyres which sent her toppling forward, almost hitting the windscreen. She recovered, fumblingly undid her seatbelt and turned to get out. Gil's hand shot out, seized her arm in an iron grip.

'I'm not marrying you!' he snarled. 'Do you understand? Whatever happens, however bad the publicity, I am not being stampeded into a shotgun wedding.'

CHAPTER NINE

HER father opened the door before Caro reached it. 'What time of night do you call this? What's going on between you and Martell? I know I told you to be nice to him, but I didn't mean——'

She wouldn't, couldn't let him finish that sentence. 'Be quiet, Dad!' she shouted, still anguished by the last thing Gil had said to her. Surely he didn't really believe she had rung that photographer in the hope of making Gil marry her? Hurt, ashamed, full of self-hatred, she turned it all on her father, her grey eyes glittering with tears. 'You had no right to ring my friends, checking up on me as if I were a schoolgirl—asking where I was, who was with me... Didn't it occur to you what sort of rumours you might start?'

'Don't you talk to me like that, my girl!' Fred muttered, his brows heavy. 'I was worried about you, after Amy rang——'

'Amy rang you?' she repeated, eyes widening. 'You didn't ring Amy, then?' That put a different complexion on it.

'No, she rang me.' Her little outburst had oddly done something to calm her father's temper. He was watching her as if puzzled, and Caro knew she was acting unusually; she had never defied her father before, never shouted at him, they had always had a good relationship. 'She woke me up, in fact,' Fred expanded. 'I'd gone to bed at half-past ten, I was tired. It must have been around one in the morning when Amy rang.'

Caro walked into the sitting-room and sank on to a chair, frowning. 'But why? Why did she ring?'

'She wanted to talk to you, she said. I wasn't best pleased, being woken up at that hour, and I told her so. Ringing people in the middle of the night! It isn't done, Amy, my love, I said, it's very thoughtless of you. But she said she was worried, you had left the party early and she thought she might have offended you somehow or other. I told her you weren't back yet and she seemed surprised. She said you had left hours ago, but then maybe you had stopped somewhere for a late supper at a nightclub, and forgotten the time.' Fred Ramsgate gestured to a flask standing on a table. 'There's some tea in there—I just had some, it's hot, do you want a cup?'

'Thanks, Dad,' she said absently, and he poured her some; she nursed the cup in both hands, glad of the warmth.

'Are you OK, Caro?' her father asked uncertainly, scratching his chin where it was rough with stubble.

'Yes, Dad,' she said, and smiled waveringly at him. She couldn't go on resenting the way he'd over-reacted; she understood and she was grateful that he cared enough to be worried.

'Well, I don't know...' mumbled Fred. 'Times like these, I wish more than ever that your mother was here. A girl needs a woman's advice; a man can't always say the right thing, ask the right questions.'

'You do OK, Dad,' she said with a loving look, and he relaxed a little.

'Well, so long as nothing's wrong—but if you're going to be out late, I wish you'd ring me...you're a grown woman, I know that, I didn't need to be told that by Martell, but I do like to know where you are and to be sure you're safe.'

'I know, I'm sorry I forgot, it won't happen again,' Caro promised, but her mind was busy with other thoughts. Was it Amy who had tipped off the photographers? But why? What possible motive could she have? Surely Amy hadn't been jealous over Gil? Well, not that jealous, anyway. Not jealous enough to do such a spiteful thing to her oldest friend? Caro drank some of the weak, milky tea, and yawned. She was so tired she could cry.

'Off to bed with you!' her father said with rough affection, now completely back to his usual good-tempered self. He took her empty cup. 'You're dead on your feet. As it's Sunday morning, you can sleep as late as you like, though.'

'Goodnight, Dad,' she said, yawning again, yet once she was in bed she couldn't get to sleep because she kept remembering the events of the night. It had been a crowded night; she shut her eyes with a muffled groan, mentally reliving it. She hadn't believed herself capable of such desire; she was hot just thinking about it. She had practically thrown herself at him. How could she have acted that way? Her father had looked at her so strangely, as though reading something in her face. Did she look very different? She felt it.

She gave up trying to sleep at about eight-thirty. Her father was nowhere to be seen; he was probably catching up on his lost night's sleep. Fred had always been able to nap whenever it suited him. Caro took a cool shower, dressed in a blue tracksuit, without bothering to put on make-up or do more than brush her hair back, then went jogging through the park. There were rarely many people about at that hour on a Sunday; a few dog-walkers, a few children and the odd jogger, like herself, loping along the wide paths between the grass and trees.

This morning the spring air had the sparkle of champagne; the lake gleamed very blue below the blue sky, there was dew on the lawns, and distances had a gentle bluish haze which held deep tranquillity.

None of which matched the turmoil inside herself, but she had learnt to outrun her demons so she set a steady pace around the lake, head up, body moving rhythmically, and while she ran she thought about her problems, all of which in the end came down to one man. Gil Martell. Her life had been peaceful until she met him; now it was like living in the eye of a storm and she didn't know what to do about it, or what she wanted to do about it.

She drew level with the park entrance near her home after her first lap of the lake, and out of the corner of her eye caught sight of a familiar shape. Her heart missed a beat, then she laughed at herself. London was full of Rolls-Royce limousines. Gil would be in bed at this moment, fast asleep.

She ran on, her skin glowing with the exercise, and was several hundred yards further on when she heard someone behind her shouting.

Caro instinctively glanced back, and saw Gil, in jeans and a white sweater, coming after her at speed, his long legs covering the ground faster than she could. He was waving a crumpled newspaper, he was obviously in one of his rages, and her heart sank.

'I want to talk to you!' he shouted. 'Stop running!'

But she ran faster, the adrenalin pumping round her body. She should have known she couldn't outrun him. He caught up with her on a lonely stretch of the path, out of sight of the lake, behind some great beech trees, and grabbed her by the waist, forcing her to stop.

The breath sobbing in her lungs, Caro leaned on him. Gil was out of breath, too. His black hair tossed in the wind, his freshly shaved skin full of colour, he glared down at her.

'Where on earth do you get your energy? You were up half the night, like me. I feel dead, but here you are, jogging in the park at about ninety miles an hour.'

'I was doing a very easy pace until you started chasing me! And what are you doing here now anyway!'

'I couldn't sleep,' he said shortly, and she looked down, watching him through her lashes, wishing she knew him better, understood him, could guess what he was thinking.

'Neither could I.' He had made an admission. So did she, and they looked at each other in silence for a moment, their breathing fast, but then Gil's black brows met and he pushed the crumpled newspaper at her.

'I got up and made myself some coffee, started to read the Sunday papers, and saw this.'

Caro reluctantly took the paper; it was one of the popular tabloids, the one which, she remembered, had carried that other photograph, of Gil and the Earl brawling in a nightclub over Miranda. She had a fleeting sense of *déjà vu*; she remembered so vividly seeing Gil's dark face for the first time in that picture and feeling that instant tug of attraction. It hadn't entered her head, of course, that before much longer she would be sharing the limelight of the national Press with him, but there she was, on the front page, with Gil, last night, outside his home.

Caught by the flash her face showed panic, and to her horror her breasts were clearly visible above the neckline of that low-cut dress, and somehow that slit in the skirt had blown back, exposing a long, shapely thigh.

'I look terrible!' she moaned. Gil looked as sexy as ever, except that he was scowling, of course, and throwing a hand up in a vain attempt to shield them both from the camera.

'Is that all you've got to say?' he snarled. 'If you're fishing for compliments, don't bother. How you look isn't the issue here. It's that headline.'

The big black headline jumped out at her. 'STORE HEIR PLAYBOY TO WED TAKEOVER GIRL' she read with horror.

'Did you give them that story?' Gil demanded.

'Of course not!' She read the copy under the picture with frantic and dismayed haste. They had it all there, in a garbled form, of course, but close enough to the truth to be difficult to deny.

'Caroline Ramsgate, only daughter of empire-building store-owner Fred Ramsgate, last night announced her engagement to Gil Martell, tycoon playboy and heir to the famous Oxford Street store, Westbrooks, which he manages for his grandmother, Lady Westbrook. Is it just coincidence that Fred Ramsgate is currently negotiating to buy Westbrooks? Or could the price of love be another major department store for the Ramsgates without any actual money changing hands? And what does Miranda, Countess of Jurby, until very recently Gil Martell's frequent companion, think about the sudden, surprising switch of his affections?'

Gil was watching Caro coldly. 'Charming, isn't it?'

'To both of us,' she agreed, her mouth twisting. 'If we *were* getting married it would be very hurtful, too. Lucky that we're not.'

'Luck has nothing to do with it,' Gil muttered, scowling. 'If I ever marry it will be because I want a woman around for life, and not for any other reason.'

He shot her a hard stare. 'Sure you didn't drop a hint to these people?'

'I told you I didn't!' she snapped. He was saying again that he wouldn't marry her for worlds, and she felt like bursting into tears, but she couldn't, so she snarled at him instead. 'But I'm pretty sure I know who did, and I think you know, too. Miranda.'

'Why should she?'

'A jealous woman is capable of anything,' Caro said, with an irony she hoped he wouldn't suspect. Her own jealousy was like a lead weight on her chest. 'Look, I can't see who else it could be. Except, maybe, your housekeeper...'

'Mrs Greybury is so discreet she thinks twice about telling me anything!' Gil said drily. 'No, it can't possibly have been her.'

'Then it's Miranda. Unless she told somebody, who tipped off the papers. But the leak had to come through Miranda.'

Gil pushed his hands into his pockets, moodily kicking the level turf they stood on. 'I suppose you're right.' He glared at her. 'Why in heaven's name did you have to tell her we were engaged? If you hadn't invented that crazy story, this wouldn't have happened.'

'You asked me to help get rid of her!'

'Well, don't give me any more of your help! You always make things worse.'

'Oh, thanks,' she said, grey eyes bright with hurt.

Gil looked into her eyes and she hurriedly looked down, her lower lip trembling. He gave a long sigh. 'I'm sorry, don't look like that! I'm just so sick of finding myself in cheap newspapers; they tell nothing but lies, but you can never prove they're lying and it's maddening.'

'That's no excuse for taking it out on me!' she said, turning away. 'Can I finish my run now, or have you got something even nastier to say to me?'

He put a hand on her arm. 'Caro——'

She slapped his hand down. 'Keep your hands off me!'

That was a mistake; it was a red rag to a bull and Gil breathed heavily, going dark red. 'You seemed to like my hands on you last night!'

Caro was so angry that her hand automatically came up to hit him. The blow didn't reach its target because Gil caught her wrist in mid-air and dragged it down-wards, dragging the rest of her with it, with such force that her body slammed into his, the impact leaving her breathless. Before she could get her breath back, Gil kissed her.

Her knees turned to jelly, her eyes closed; she kissed him back with helpless yearning for just an instant, then her mind began screaming and she woke up and realised what she was doing. She opened her eyes and saw that Gil had his eyes shut, which made her feel very odd again, for a second, then she used all her strength to pull free and began to run.

She thought he would follow her, and her heart was beating like a tom-tom, but he didn't. She didn't look back to see what he did, but as she jogged along beside the lake a few minutes later she glanced across the water and saw through the trees that the Rolls had gone. She told herself she was relieved, but she wasn't sure if she was telling the truth.

She went home twenty minutes later, showered again, got dressed in a simple but chic olive-green dress and went down to get some breakfast only to find that her father was up, eating his own breakfast, with that news-paper spread out on the table in front of him.

Caro stopped dead and Fred Ramsgate turned his head to stare at her. 'Is this true?' He looked stunned.

Very flushed, Caro shook her head. 'No, Dad. You should know what newspapers are like, they invent most of their gossip.' She sat down opposite him and poured herself a cup of tea from the heavy silver teapot in the centre of the table. She didn't eat a cooked breakfast, merely slid a slice of wholemeal bread into the toaster, very aware of her father's eyes watching her every move.

'Well, where on earth did they get it?' he not unnaturally demanded. 'What put the idea into their heads? The financial pages have run speculation about a possible take-over of Westbrooks, that isn't surprising, but why did they dream up an engagement between you and Martell?'

'Well... You see, Gil was being harassed by Miranda—the Countess of——'

'I remember her! Get on with it!' Fred said grumpily, watching her spread her toast with marmalade. 'What do you mean, harassed by her? What was she doing?'

'Whenever she quarrels with her husband she tries to move in with Gil, and he asked me to help get rid of her.'

Fred grunted disapproval. 'Chivalrous of him!'

Caro contrarily resented the criticism of Gil, although she had herself been irritated with him over the way he seemed incapable of dealing with Miranda. 'He didn't want her to keep involving him in her marital problems,' she defended uneasily. 'The newspaper gossip was all lies, both she and her husband are very old, close friends of his, there's no love-affair going on between her and Gil, but she would run to him whenever she quarrelled with her husband, and he wanted her to stop.'

'He could have tried telling her how he felt,' Fred said drily. 'If they're such old, close friends, surely he can talk frankly to her?'

'She wouldn't listen,' Caro said with a sudden flare of rage. 'She's the most spoilt, selfish, unreasonable——' She broke off, knowing she had given herself away and her father eyed her with frowning concern. She looked down, very flushed. 'It was her who gave that story to the Press, out of spite! You see, I . . . well, it seemed a good idea at the time . . . it was just on impulse . . . I told her Gil and I were engaged. I thought she would go away then, and she did, but she must have told the newspaper and they had a photographer outside Gil's flat, and . . .' She gestured to the paper. 'There you are!'

Fred put down his cup with a clatter, almost spilling the tea. 'I can't believe my daughter could do anything so stupid! What on earth possessed you? What did Martell have to say?' His eyes narrowed, and sharp suspicion darted through his face. 'Or was it really his idea? He got you to tell her you were engaged to him, then he leaks it to the papers, and hey, presto! It has to become a fact. Oh, yes, I can see how it would be a very attractive prospect for him. He's a very shrewd fellow, he knows that when I take over I'll change all the top management there, which means he will lose his job, and he must have been going crazy trying to work out how to stop that. If he married you, he wouldn't lose Westbrooks, he would be my son-in-law, with a glittering future in front of him——'

'No!' Caro almost shouted; she was shaking with pain and rage. 'It was my idea, and Gil was furious with me, he's still furious. You don't know him, he isn't the type to marry for money, in fact, he told me so—he said he wouldn't marry me if——' She broke off, swallowing, unable to meet her father's intent eyes, afraid of what he must be picking up.

It was a relief when the phone on the sideboard behind her began to shrill. She picked it up, thinking that if it was the Press she would just hang up. It wasn't. It was Lady Westbrook, sounding elated.

'Oh, hello, Lady Westbrook,' Caro said warily.

'My dear girl, what wonderful news! I am so happy. I couldn't be more pleased. From the minute I met you, I felt instinctively that you were the wife I have always wanted for Gil, a nice girl with a kind heart and good manners, and a sound head on her shoulders.'

She sounded satisfied with that description, but Caro wasn't—she had to bite her lip because it made her sound so unutterably dull. But she had to explain to Lady Westbrook that she was not engaged to Gil, that the newspaper story was lies. So she took a deep breath, hunting for the right words, and while she was doing so Lady Westbrook happily chattered on.

'But why didn't you tell me? Why did I have to find out from a newspaper, heaven help us? Your father knew, I suppose?' There was distinct chagrin in her voice—she was an old woman whose feelings had been hurt, and Caro was sorry about that; she liked Gil's grandmother, so without stopping to think she hurriedly reassured her.

'Oh, no, Dad knew nothing about it!'

Fred Ramsgate, who had been eavesdropping, leaned over and took the telephone away. 'I certainly did not! I'm furious.'

Caro didn't hear what Lady Westbrook replied, but it made her father laugh before giving the phone back to her. He might not like the idea of Gil as a husband for his daughter, but, as Caro knew, he was very impressed by Lady Westbrook.

'Why ever did you tell Miranda first?' Lady Westbrook asked. 'And then let it break in the Press before you told us? I really don't understand young people, they behave in the strangest way, but never mind, I forgive you. I would forgive anything if it meant that I could die happy, knowing I was leaving Gil safely in your hands.'

'Oh, please, I'm sorry, but you see I——' Caro broke in, distressed, but before she could tell her the truth, Lady Westbrook cut across her.

'My dear girl, it doesn't matter. All that matters is that you and Gil are going to be happy, which makes me very happy indeed. Now, I want to see you both, to give you my blessing. I don't know what Gil was thinking of doing about an engagement ring, but it would make me very happy indeed if you would wear mine. Do you remember it? I must have been wearing it when you came to dinner—a big ruby set with diamonds? Come to dinner tonight, you and Gil, but of course I would like your father there, too. A family party.'

'Oh, dear, but . . . you see, I'm sorry, we can't,' Caro unhappily began. 'Lady Westbrook, I have to tell you——'

Lady Westbrook didn't wait for her to get the right words out; she plunged on in the same high-pitched excitement. 'Never mind, how about tomorrow, then? That will give you time to break any other date you had. We have so many plans to make, we must start as soon as possible. Have you had any thoughts yet on the reception? Where do you think? How about holding it in a marquee on my lawns? You can cram hundreds into a large marquee.'

Caro made desperate, agitated noises, and finally said, 'I think you'd better talk to Gil.' Let him tell his grandmother the truth.

Lady Westbrook laughed happily. 'Oh, you don't like the idea of a marquee? Well, never mind, we'll talk tomorrow night and come up with a better one, but I'm sure Gil will like whatever you like, although it is wiser to pretend to consult your man, my dear, you're right. They like to think we want their opinion, but we don't have to do what they suggest, do we? Well, I'll look forward so much to seeing you again. And— Caroline... welcome to the family.'

Caro put the phone down, close to tears. Her father watched her, his brows low over his eyes. 'I wish I knew what was really going on here!' he said grimly. 'Are you OK, my girl? You can tell me, come on! What's wrong?'

Caro pulled herself together. 'Nothing, Dad. I'm just tired after doing that long job on the Westbrooks accounts, and then all this fuss and nonsense... and I had a sleepless night last night and...' She turned towards the door in a hurry. 'I think I'll go and write letters, and listen to some music. See you later.'

The telephone was ringing again but this time she ignored it and left it to their housekeeper to answer. It was a newspaper, she was told a moment later, wanting to speak to her, but Caro shook her head. 'Tell them I'm out. If anyone at all rings up, tell them I'm out.'

She was going to ground for the rest of the day. She had an uneasy suspicion that tomorrow was going to be a rough day. In the morning, she was attending the negotiations between the Westbrooks people and her father's lawyers and accountants. Damian Shaw would be there, but by now she felt no nervous qualm about meeting him again. It was Gil's presence she was bothered about.

When she walked into the boardroom where the meeting was taking place, the first person she saw was Gil, and her nerve-endings flickered with disturbing excitement. He was standing by the window talking to one of his grandmother's lawyers, facing the door through which she came, and he saw her at more or less the same time. Caro felt as if she had been hit by lightning when their eyes met; there was an instant flash of electricity between them.

He looked formidable and distinguished in a dark blue pin-stripe suit, his cream silk tie perfectly knotted, his shirt crisp and immaculate. He might be going to lose his store, but he meant to fight for it, and he wasn't conceding an inch of personal territory as he nodded, unsmilingly, then looked away. A stranger watching might have thought they barely knew each other, or were perhaps enemies. Perhaps they were? Caro grimly thought.

She sat down at one end of the long, polished table under the rather stolid portrait of her father, which had been presented to him by the board for his fiftieth birthday. The artist had painted her father's best suit, his gold watch-chain and tie-pin, his ruddy skin and jowled jaw, his shrewd acumen and the toughness which made him so good at business, but he hadn't dug any deeper to discover the man Caro knew. Where was Fred's earthy humour, his kindness, and the loving heart which had still not forgotten her dead mother, although so many years had gone by?

'Good morning, Caroline,' said a voice beside her and she started, looking up at Leonard Ross. Small, thin and grey, Leonard had begun working for Fred as an accountant many years ago and had progressed to a seat on the board, where he was in overall charge of the various buying departments of the stores. Leonard was an expert on the subject of costs and profits and how to lower the first and raise the second.

'Nice to see you, Leonard,' she said. 'How's Rose?'

'Oh, she's fine. She had a cold last week but she's over that.'

'And the children?'

'Children?' he said with amused derision. 'Caroline, my youngest is older than you! But they're all great, thank you for asking.' He gave her a grin. 'But what about you, then?'

'I'm great, too,' she said lightly.

'I meant how about what we've all been reading?' Leonard said cheerfully, and the room went silent; everyone seemed to turn and stare, and Caro wanted to sink through the floor. 'When we saw it in the papers, Rose and I were staggered. I had no idea you were even dating him!' He glanced round, suddenly realised how people were listening and watching them, and hurriedly concluded, 'Well, I hope you're going to be very happy, Caroline.'

Before she could answer, Gil strode to the table and dropped a pile of folders on it with a little crash. 'Shall we get started?' he said loudly, and Leonard rushed off to take his seat, as did everyone else.

Caro and Gil stared at each other along the gleaming, highly polished table, like duellists before they began to fight, a level, hostile gaze needing no words.

She had dressed carefully for this meeting, too: her smooth, tailored wool dress was black, she wore small pearl studs in her ears and a string of pearls around her neck, carried a black purse and wore fine, handmade black high-heeled shoes. She might not be pretty, but she knew she looked elegantly businesslike. She had wanted to command the respect of everyone in the room, including Gil.

Her father sat down beside her, murmuring, 'Nervous?'

She made a little face. 'Well, I don't enjoy addressing these big meetings, but I'll be fine.' A breakdown of her report, excluding anything confidential, had been circulated to them all, including Gil and his people, and she knew she was going to face rigorous questioning about it. She was sure she could hold her own, but she was bothered by the prospect of being taken apart by Gil. She knew she would either lose her temper and shout at him, or go to pieces, and she wasn't sure which she dreaded the most.

She ran her eyes over the faces around the table. Most of them men, she noted grimly, as usual. Few women seemed to get to this level. They were dominant at lower levels in the stores, but her father had packed his board with men, and most of the lawyers and accountants he employed were men, too.

That will change one day, she thought. When I'm running this business there will be a lot more women at top management level. They are allowed so far, and no further, and it's very frustrating for the most able women to keep hitting their heads against that ceiling.

Her eyes met Gil's again and quickly moved on around the table. A frown drew her brows together. One face was missing. She checked again, then murmured to her father, 'I thought Damian Shaw was going to be here?'

Her father gave her an odd look. Did he imagine she was dying to see Damian? He knew she had once been in love with him, years ago, and had been badly hurt. 'It seems he no longer works for Gil,' Fred said carefully.

Caro stiffened and shot a look down the table to where Gil was reading a thick file of papers. What had happened? Had he fired Damian? Or had Damian walked out? Her mind seethed with questions but Fred was banging on the table with a wooden gavel to get everyone's attention, and Caro heard him begin to introduce her.

'You all know my daughter, Caroline.' Fred's voice was jovial. 'And I've no doubt you've all read the latest piece of exciting fiction published by the so-called gentlemen of the Press.' Everyone laughed, except Caro and Gil, both of whom stared at the table. Fred went on, 'But we're not here to talk about that. We're here to discuss the report she has put together on Westbrooks. The final negotiations will be based on her findings, so this is a vital document, and I hope you all know it backwards.'

Caro stood up to polite applause and began her brief outline of the report as they had all read it. 'Now, if you have any questions I shall be happy to answer them,' she ended, sitting down.

A silence fell. Everyone on the Westbrooks team looked at Gil. He was leaning back in his chair, his dark eyes fixed on the ceiling, his fingers silently tapping on the polished table. He seemed to be lost in thought.

After a moment or two, one of the accountants asked Caro a question about the projected profit graph on the back of the report.

She answered readily, and several other questions came hot on the heels of that, none of them difficult or hard to answer. After around twenty minutes it was obvious that Gil either had nothing to say, or was reserving his fire, and Caro grew very edgy. What was he up to? Why was he staying silent? She kept waiting for him to intervene, to start his cross-examination of her, but he did not make a move. Everyone around the table was clearly intrigued; they kept glancing at each other, lifting their brows or grinning, and Caro knew what they were thinking. Gil's silence had led them to believe that the sale of Westbrooks no longer had any importance for him because he was marrying her anyway, and would remain in control of the store.

But that wasn't true. Gil had told her furiously that he wasn't marrying her to keep his store. No shotgun wedding, he had said, and he had meant it. So why was he staying silent?

Fred looked at his watch a few moments later. 'Any more questions?' There was a significant pause, everyone looked at the table, then Fred said, 'Well, if no one has any further questions for my daughter, I suggest we break for coffee now.'

Caro gathered up her papers, smiled politely at the congratulations people offered her, then said quietly to her father, 'Do you want me any more after the break, Dad?'

'Stay if you want to, or not, as you like,' Fred said.

'I think I'll get back to my office,' she said. 'I have a mound of paperwork I've had to neglect while I did this report.'

Everyone was crowding round the far end of the room, where the coffee was laid out. Caro was able to slip out without being noticed, and spent the rest of the day in her office working with angry energy. She worked late. Her father was to be a guest at an important dinner in the City of London, at which the main speaker was to be the Prime Minister, so she did not have to get home in time to eat dinner with Fred. She wasn't hungry, and couldn't be bothered to go out for a meal. Their house-keeper was off for the evening, too, so Caro decided that when she did get home she would have beans on toast or scrambled egg, cooked by herself and eaten at the kitchen table.

It was nearly nine when she let herself into the house. Silence lay on it like dust; sometimes she was disturbed by being alone in a house but not tonight. Tonight, she needed to be alone. She felt like someone after a fu-neral: haunted by loss, heavy with grief.

She walked slowly towards the kitchen. Just as she was opening the door she heard a crash from one of the other rooms and froze. What was that?

Hadn't Fred gone to that dinner? But if he hadn't, he would have rung to tell her he would be at home. He had known she was working late.

She stood listening intently, her nerves stretched, and heard another sound, a faint movement.

There was someone in the house, in the sitting-room. She crept back along the hall to listen outside the door, and heard somebody breathing on the other side of the door. Were they listening to her? If only she had a weapon! She looked around frantically, saw a heavy walking-stick of her father's with a silver handle, and grabbed it. That would do!

She took a deep breath, quietly turned the handle of the sitting-room door and gave a rapid glance around, and saw a man with his back to her, actually having the nerve to pour himself a glass of her father's best whisky. Caro leapt at him, the heavy stick raised.

He heard her coming and whirled, jumping aside just in time before the silver handle would have come down on his skull.

'What the devil do you think you're doing?'

Caro dropped the stick, turning white, then red. 'Gil! I could have killed you!'

CHAPTER TEN

GIL bent to retrieve the stick and weighed it in his hand, grimacing. 'I'm very glad that didn't smash into my head! You're a dangerous woman.' He glanced at her through his lashes, smiling crookedly. 'But then I knew that.'

'I thought you were a burglar!' Caro whispered with an enormous effort. She was feeling very odd; waves of coldness were washing over her. She swayed and the room went round and round. Oh, no, I'm going to faint, she thought, panic-stricken. I can't ... not now ... not with Gil watching me ...

The next time she opened her eyes she was lying on a couch and Gil was kneeling beside her, pushing back the hair from her forehead, staring anxiously at her. 'Caro...' he said huskily. 'You scared the life out of me. Are you OK?'

'I fainted,' she said with bitterness. Gil was always seeing her in embarrassing situations. What a fool he must think her!

'Right into my arms,' he said, stroking her cheek with the tips of his fingers, and his caress made her head swim again. She sat up hurriedly, very flushed now, her body was always going from one extreme to the other while Gil Martell was around.

'Gil, how did you get into the house? What are you doing here?' she asked, brushing down her skirt and running a shaky hand over her dishevelled hair.

'Your father and I had drinks together here—a private celebration.'

'My father's here?' Caro looked around vaguely and Gil shook his head.

'Not now, he had to go to a dinner in the City. I waited for you to come home.'

'Why?' she asked, then, suddenly afraid, asked another question more urgently, 'Celebration? Celebration of what?'

'The successful outcome of the negotiations. It's all over bar the actual signing of the contract. Your father has added Westbrooks to his empire. My grandmother accepted his price and we all shook hands on it, then I came back here with your father and we had a couple of drinks together.'

'And the price?' Caro asked, wondering if her father had had to offer more than he originally had. The store would be a good buy, even so. It was seriously undervalued.

Gil grinned at her. 'Oh, that sharp little accountant's brain! I can see you've recovered from your passing weakness.' He looked sideways at her and her heart missed a beat. What did that mean? He smoothly added, 'Well, my grandmother took my advice——'

'Your advice?' Caro interrupted, her eyes alert. Gil had been violently opposed to the deal. What had he advised his grandmother to do?

'Yes, I thought your father's offer was pitched too low. Your report made it quite clear that there was amazing potential for future growth. I was very impressed. You're a formidable opponent, Caroline Ramsgate.'

'Thank you,' she said, not sure how to take that. Was it a compliment or a criticism? 'So what was the price?'

'We asked for a five-per-cent increase in the price——'

'What? And my father gave it to you?' She was incredulous. That took the price a couple of million above what they had been offering. Surely her father hadn't agreed to that?

'No, but he agreed to a three-per-cent increase, since we were offering a further property.'

Confused, she frowned. 'What do you mean? What further property?'

'Me,' Gil said.

Her head spun and she stared, eyes wide and startled. 'You? What are you talking about?'

'Your father bought me,' Gil said, and hot colour rushed up Caro's face.

'That isn't funny!'

Gil laughed shortly. 'No, it isn't—and your father hasn't bought me, either, although he thinks he has. I didn't bother to disabuse him of the notion, he seemed too happy about it. Oh, don't look like that! I like your father. He's quite lovable, in his way, monster though he is—but it's time he realised his money can't buy everything.'

'I don't know what you're talking about,' Caro said, getting up impatiently and facing him.

Gil got to his feet lazily and looked down at her with mocking dark eyes. 'Your father and I had lunch together and talked. That was when he made his astounding offer. He had decided you wanted me, it seems, and whatever his darling daughter wants she has to have, so he told me to name my own price. Literally.'

'I don't believe you!' Caro whispered, but she did, burning with rage against her father. Oh, how could he?

What on earth had possessed him to do such a shameful thing?

'When I told him that I liked to do my own proposing and I wasn't in the market to be bought up by prospective father-in-laws, he flew into a temper,' Gil drily said. 'He became very Victorian, and said I had compromised you. He was apparently incensed by the story that appeared in yesterday's paper. More by the picture, I gathered, and the implications of it. You had been photographed with me coming out of my home in the early hours of the morning, in a very dishevelled state, and the whole world was going to believe that we had been sleeping together.' He looked at her through his lashes, smiling crookedly, and Caro couldn't stop the inevitable rise in her colour. Did he have to keep reminding her? As if she needed reminding! Images of their lovemaking kept flashing through her head when she least wanted them; she was haunted by those moments in his arms.

'I'm sorry, it's ridiculous, I'll speak to my father,' she said stiffly.

Gil did not seem to be listening. He slid a hand inside his jacket pocket and produced a small, square, velvet-covered box. She stared at it as if it were a snake and might bite her. He opened it on a dazzle of red and white; she remembered the ring as soon as she saw it.

'This was my grandmother's engagement ring,' he said, raising it so that the facets of the great ruby flamed in the light, the little diamonds around it glittering. 'She wants you to wear it, but if you'd rather have a new ring...'

'No,' she said involuntarily, her eyes on the ruby. 'It's beautiful.' Then she pulled herself together. 'I'm not marrying you!' she told him. How could she, now? How could her father do this to her?

'Well,' he said doubtfully, his dark head on one side as he contemplated her, 'we could live together, of course, without bothering to get married, but I shudder to think of the Press coverage we'd get. No, much simpler to get married. Far less fuss in the long run.'

'You told me you weren't going to be stampeded into a shotgun wedding!' she bitterly reminded him. 'What changed your mind? What exactly did my father offer you? That you would remain in control at Westbrooks?'

'Yes,' he agreed coolly.

Her blood turned to ice; a sliver of it seemed to reach her heart and she wanted to die. 'And you claim you can't be bought?' she spat at him.

'I didn't say I'd accepted.' Gil suddenly seized her hand and deftly slid the ruby and diamond ring up her ring finger. 'It's a pretty good fit, oddly enough,' he said in some surprise. 'I thought it might be too big, but my grandmother's hands must be more or less the same size as yours.'

Caro stared dumbly at the deep red glow against her pale skin. The ruby seemed to pulse while she gazed into it, and she loved the weight of it, the beauty of it, on her hand, but she shook her head, pulling free of Gil and taking the ring off.

'No, I can't marry you,' she said, offering him the ring.

He took it and put it back into the box without argument. 'I'm leaving next month,' he murmured and Caro frowned.

'Leaving? Westbrooks?'

'Yes, Westbrooks—and the country.' He sat down again on the couch, and Caro automatically sat down, too, stunned by what he had just said.

'You're going abroad? A holiday?'

He shook his head, leaned back and crossed his legs casually. 'No, I've accepted a job in California, running a new department store in Beverly Hills. It's an exciting project, a new concept in shopping, but I can't talk about that yet, it's all very hush-hush in case the opposition steal a march on us. The building is almost complete, but we won't be opening until the autumn, which gives me plenty of time to get my operation in place.'

Caro swallowed, her throat hurting. He was going away. Gil was leaving the country, going thousands of miles away, to the west cost of America. She might never see him again. 'If you've accepted this new job, why did you go through that pantomime of asking me to marry you, offering me that ring...?' she muttered harshly. 'Was that some sort of joke? You must have a weird sense of humour if you found that funny!'

'Watch me laugh,' he said, turning his face to her, and as she looked into those dark eyes her body began to shake and she couldn't breathe. Gil's hand caught her arm and dragged her towards him. At the first touch of his mouth she was burning, her body on fire as she clung, kissing him hungrily. Gil had both arms round her now, and they toppled and fell from the couch to the floor, without the kiss ending. Caro almost lost all sense of her identity; she was consumed with passion, and only when Gil broke the kiss did she slowly come back to consciousness, lifting dazed eyes to his flushed face.

'I love you,' Gil said hoarsely.

Caro couldn't believe what he had said; tears came into her eyes, she shut them, shaking her head.

'Yes,' Gil said. 'I don't know why or how, I think it started the day I saw you in that fitting-room at Westbrooks. You have a very sexy body and I couldn't take my eyes off it.'

She remembered that, blushing. 'Or your hands,' she said.

'Or my hands,' Gil agreed, laughing huskily. 'I wanted you. I've wanted other women, of course...'

She looked coldly at him. 'I know.'

He laughed, his eyes tender. 'You terrifying woman! OK, there have been other women, I like women and they usually like me, but I never even considered marrying any of them. I liked my freedom too much, I was having too good a time.'

'And they didn't have fathers as rich as mine?' Caro bitterly accused.

'If I told you that didn't matter a row of beans to me, would you believe me?' he asked and she shook her head. 'Then I won't bother.' He shrugged, his mouth hard. 'If you don't trust me enough to marry me, OK. We won't get married.'

She sat up, shakily pushing her hair back from her face. 'Gil, how can I trust you when I know the sort of women you've always dated? I read the gossip columns, I've seen Miranda. She's beautiful, I expect they all were. I'm not.'

He put a hand under her chin and turned her reluctant face to him, contemplating it thoughtfully. 'No, you're not.'

She hadn't expected him to lie, but she hated hearing the truth from him, and her grey eyes blazed. Gil grinned at her, his long index finger flicking down her cheek.

'What a temper you've got! Did you want me to say you were beautiful? We're going to tell the truth to each other, Caro, it's the only way we can live together. Your face isn't beautiful, but your body is magnificent.' He watched the rise of her colour, laughing. 'It really turns me on,' he whispered, and she wanted so badly to believe him, but she still couldn't forget Miranda.

'That isn't any reason for marrying,' she muttered and he agreed.

'No, and if you can't trust me there would be no point in getting married, either. We could still live together, couldn't we?'

Caro's whole body jerked in shock. 'Live together?'

'Come to America with me, we'll build this new store together. You understand how to run a store, I've never met anyone who had a mind like yours. If I weren't in love with you I'd want to employ you, you're worth your weight in gold.'

She had been angry when he'd told her he loved her because she'd been sure he was lying, but she was flattered now because she knew she was good at her job—she could believe Gil when he said she understood how to run a store. It was true. She did. She had spent most of her life listening to her father, working in stores, thinking about ways to run them, arguing with her father about her ideas and often being frustrated because if their ideas clashed it was Fred Ramsgate's plans which went ahead while hers were pushed aside.

'My father would go crazy,' she said slowly, imagining her father's face.

'Let him. I'm not scared of your father,' Gil said, shrugging.

'Neither am I!' she protested. 'But I love him and I don't want to hurt him or make him angry. If I leave him and go to work for you, he won't understand, he'll be knocked for six.'

Gil's dark eyes were hard, glittering. 'It's a difficult choice for you, then. I guessed it would be—I've realised how much your father has always dominated you, and I'm not prepared to let him go on dictating your life, Caro, not if we're going to be together from now on. It's either him or me. You can't belong to us both.'

Her heart hurt her at the thought of belonging to Gil. Could she bear to lose him? Even if she didn't quite believe he meant what he said about loving her, could she bear to see him go away to the other side of the earth, when he was offering to take her with him? But the thought of explaining all this to her father! She flinched from the prospect. Fred would be so furious. His daughter, living with a man she hadn't married, working for him rather than for her own father! She could imagine his face. Fred had solid, old-fashioned, immovable ideas. He believed in marriage and family. He thought she owed him all her loyalty, as his daughter. He had trained her, she should repay him. Fred was firmly rooted in an earlier time, and she had always loved him for that, for the stability and security, the unfailing affection he had always given her.

She was tired after a very long, arduous day—it wasn't easy to think clearly. Her thoughts kept dissolving into chaos. But how would she ever know Gil really wanted her? What about Miranda? What about his resentment over her father's buying Westbrooks? She remembered that tense meeting in the boardroom; Gil's face whenever she looked at him. A new thought suddenly occurred to her, a question she had been meaning to ask him—and she asked it then.

'Gil, why wasn't Damian Shaw at the meeting this morning?'

Gill stiffened visibly. 'Why? Were you looking forward to seeing him again?' he asked with roughness in his voice.

'No,' she said mildly, watching him. 'But I had expected to—where was he?'

'I told him I didn't need him any more.' Gil's face was dark red, he looked irritable. Caro's heart missed a beat.

'Why did you do that?'

'I can't stand the man,' Gil said through his teeth, and she felt a strange breathlessness.

'Don't pretend you were jealous!'

Gil laughed shortly. 'Jealous? Nothing of the kind. My decision had nothing to do with you at all. I just decided I didn't want him working for me any more.'

He was lying now. She was sure of it. Gil was jealous. He wasn't faking that look; she saw the black glitter of his eyes and knew it was genuine.

'After the way he cheated you, you'd have to be insane to want to see him again, anyway,' Gil bit out, and she was absolutely certain then. Gil had got rid of Damian because he was afraid she might still be interested in him.

That didn't mean Gil loved her, of course, but it did mean that Gil wasn't sure of her. He didn't know, for sure, that she loved him, as Caro had been afraid he did. Of course, it might merely mean that Gil wanted no rivals around because he planned to marry her for her father's money, as Damian had wanted to do. Her brows met. The comparison was crazy—Gil Martell was no Damian. She knew Gil so well now. He wasn't the same type at all. Damian had been smooth and charming. Gil was neither. He was direct, outspoken to the point of being rude, and infuriating. How could she ever have even considered the idea of Gil's being another Damian?

Gil had watched her, his face dark. 'You don't still think about him, do you, Caro?' he asked uncertainly, and she smiled at him, shaking her head.

'Only with distaste.'

Gil's face cleared and he laughed. 'Well, that's a relief.' He held out his hand. 'Come with me, Caro,' he said huskily, and she wished she had the courage to say yes without even hesitating. She wanted him so much, she would die if she couldn't have him. She took a long, painful breath and then she slowly put her hand in his, sighing.

'I must be mad.'

Gil bent his dark head and kissed her hand. 'No, darling, you're the sanest person I've ever met, and I love you.' He pulled her into his arms and sought her mouth, breathing her name softly. 'I love you,' he said again, kissing her, and Caro said it back passionately.

'I love you, Gil...'

She felt his body tremble, felt the wild beating of his heart against her, and happiness made her want to sing, because she believed him suddenly. His body couldn't lie to her; the hunger surging in it was as true as the earth beneath her feet. Gil loved her. He loved her.

They flew to California a fortnight later. Fred and Lady Westbrook saw them off, neither of them very happy. From the viewpoint of their generation, Gil and Caro were behaving disgracefully.

'But if you love each other enough to live together,' Lady Westbrook said unhappily, 'why not get married first?'

'We can always get married last, if we decide that's what we want,' Gil said, holding Caro's hand, which was trembling slightly because she hated this sort of family wrangle and she hated having made the older pair unhappy.

'Caro, dear, are you sure this is what you want?' Lady Westbrook appealed to her, and she nodded, managing a smile.

'I'm sure.' She wanted to be certain Gil loved her, and if they married now she would never be sure.

'But if you don't marry, you won't have children, and I want great-grandchildren,' the old woman quavered.

'In good time,' Gil said, grinning at Caro, who looked at him uncertainly. They had not even discussed having children. As they would be fully occupied with their working lives, children had not been on their list of priorities.

'Caro, I can't believe you're really going to leave me and go to work for other people,' Fred accused, his lower lip stuck out in a childish pout. 'Why go to America to work for strangers, when you can work for our own firm?'

He had harped on that theme ever since she and Gil had told him their plans. 'Dad, it does no harm to get experience of another firm, does it?' she gently asked.

'But what can they teach you that I haven't already taught you?' he muttered.

He had already asked that, too, over and over again. He had said other things, too, bitter, furious things about Gil's reasons for taking her to America. 'He wants revenge on me, for taking Westbrooks away from him,' Fred had said. 'I offered him the management of the store, but he refused, turned me down flat—why? Because he wants to hit back at me, and he knows he can do that through you. He isn't marrying you, is he? If he loves you, why doesn't he marry you?'

'He did ask me, but I decided to wait,' Caro had said again, as she had already said a dozen times before. Her father was perfectly happy to repeat himself forever if it finally got him his own way. He had learnt patience and tenacity in a hard school, in his youth, and he believed that if you only said something often enough it could wear away all opposition, like water dropping on a stone.

'Our marriage will be a private affair, not a business deal, some sort of shotgun wedding with Gil forced to marry me to keep Westbrooks, or me forced to marry him to satisfy your ideas of how I ought to behave,' she had added once, her face angry. 'It's my life, Dad, not yours. When I'm certain we're happy together and want to be together for the rest of our lives, I'll marry him.'

'I don't understand you any more,' Fred had said grimly, and he looked grim now, staring at her in the crowded airport terminal, as if he wished he knew what had happened to his daughter to turn her into a stranger.

'We'll be back, Dad,' she said affectionately, kissing his cheek. 'Don't look so worried. We don't plan to stay over there forever, just for a couple of years, to get the new store up and running.'

Gil took her hand, holding it tightly. 'It's going to be tremendous fun, working together out there, on a project like this,' he said, smiling at the older couple. 'Come out and visit us soon, you'll be fascinated, Fred. We'll be glad to see you any time.'

Their flight was called and they said their last farewells. Lady Westbrook clung to Gil, tears in her eyes. 'I'll miss you...'

'I'll see you often,' he promised.

She kissed Caro, hugged her. 'Take care of him for me.'

Caro nodded. 'Don't worry, I will.' She turned to give her father a last kiss, whispering, 'I love you, Dad, look after yourself...'

'You, too,' Fred muttered, and then Gil and Caro walked away, hand in hand, pausing only to look back and wave before they vanished through to the departure lounge.

As their plane headed away from London through a hot May sky, Caro leaned back in her seat, watching the city stream away below them, thinking back to the first time she had ever seen Gil, and how she had felt, the strange, bewildering turmoil of her feelings even then. She had seen him as dangerous to her, from the start; she had learnt to fear loving because one man had hurt her years ago, and she had seen in Gil at once the threat of love.

She looked sideways through her lashes at his clear-cut, familiar profile, and said huskily, 'Gil...?'

'Mmm?' he asked, sipping the glass of champagne the stewardess had brought them a moment earlier.

'I'm scared,' Caro whispered, and he turned to look quickly at her.

'Scared about coming with me?'

'Scared about being so happy,' she confessed. 'It's frightening to feel like this...'

His face cleared and he laughed, taking her hand and kissing the palm lingeringly. 'It's going to last,' he promised, his dark eyes passionate. 'I've never been so sure of anything in my life. We belong together, I think I knew it from the minute I saw you.'

Caro held his hand tightly. 'I knew too,' she said. 'That was why I was so scared.' The threat of love did terrify, like a giant wave about to envelop you, but if you threw yourself into it you suddenly found yourself able to ride the ocean and fly with the wind.

Gil smiled at her, then he looked past her into the blue, blue sky through which they flew to their unknown, shared future. 'Isn't life amazing?' he said.

my VALENTINE 1992

Celebrate the most romantic day of the year with
MY VALENTINE 1992—a sexy new collection of four
romantic stories written by our famous Temptation
authors:

GINA WILKINS
KRISTINE ROLOFSON
JOANN ROSS
VICKI LEWIS THOMPSON

My Valentine 1992—an exquisite escape into a romantic
and sensuous world.

 Harlequin Books

VAL-92-R